HOW I GOT LOST IN SPACE

Look for More Terrorlands Books
by Marco Chu Kwan Ching

TERRORLAND

HOW I GOT LOST IN SPACE

MARCO CHU KWAN CHING

A
PEAR
PAPERBACK

ISBN: 978-0-6486552-0-6

First printing in 2018
Second printing in 2019

PART 1

1

The whole world was spinning.

I tumbled into space.

The black hole behind me was like a giant monster.

I tried to swim back to the space shuttle with all my strength.

But, no matter how hard I tried, the space shuttle kept drifting further and further away from view.

It felt like an unknown current was pushing back against me in an ocean.

I struggled to swim forward.

This is no good…

It is just a matter of time before I will be completely lost in space.

I began to panic.

My heart was pounding fast.

I was breathing so hard that I could hear it.

The water vapor in my breath condensed and blurred my visor.

My hope of returning to Earth was swallowed by despair.

I really want to scream. I really want someone to come and rescue me.

But, the truth is, when you are in space, no one can hear you scream.

The oxygen level in my spacesuit continued to decline.

Nova. Stop wasting time. Quick. Think of something! I urged myself.

2

My name is Nova.

I am twelve.

Unlike most of you, I am an orphan.

I don't even remember the feeling of having parents.

Mom and Dad left me for a space mission when I turned four.

Why would they do that?

I have no idea.

They told me the wonderful thing about their mission is to terraform other planets to make them suitable for our generation to habitat.

Do you know what they were talking about?

I still don't.

I looked at the vintage family photo of my four-year-old birthday.

It had my favorite dark forest chocolate birthday cake.

Dad was lighting the birthday candles.

Mom was clapping beside him, while singing a birthday song for me.

Happy birthday to you. Happy birthday to you.

Happy birthday to Nova. Happy Birthday to you.
Hip Hip Hooray.
Mom's musical voice echoed in my thoughts.

Slowly, I drifted back into reality.

Drops of tears run down my face.

They promised me they would only be gone a short while.

They promised me they would be back for my five-year-old birthday.

But, they never did.

I hate you. I hate both of you.

I promise I will find you in space.

My last image of them was in some kind of bulky white spacesuit with a big, fat, ugly black helmet, waving good-bye to me.

I did not even get to see their face.

Ironic, isn't it?

Suddenly, my bedroom door spun open.

A shaft of light from the door gap blinded my eyes.

"Sister, Miss O' Connor is waiting for us in the assembly hall," Peter reported, catching his breath.

"All right, I am coming," I said, quickly wiping my tears and putting the photo away.

"Sister, are you all right?" Peter asked in a soft voice.

"I am fine," I insisted. "Do you want to knock next time?"

"Sorry, sister. I… I will remember," Peter apologized. "But, Miss O' Connor wants everyone to be there in five minutes."

"All right, I will be there," I replied.

Peter is ten. He has big round, blue eyes and short

blonde hair. He is a bit chubby for his age.

Like me, he is an orphan.

Maybe that is why we have so much in common.

Obviously, Peter is not my real brother. And I am not his real sister. We have been in a brother-sister relationship ever since I protected him from a bully in our school called Tommy.

Everyone in school says Peter is a nerd, but I know he isn't.

He is just smart – smarter than other students of his age.

In fact, he has been attending my astronomy class two grades above his age.

A final message ringtone from my phone interrupted my thoughts.

It was from Miss O' Connor, our orphan school principal.

I wondered why she is gathering everyone all of a sudden.

This is very unusual.

3

"Attention!"

Miss O' Connor was standing on the stage. Her voiced boomed as everyone hurried to line up in an open space assembly hall.

The boy scouts were busy raising the St. George Orphan School flag.

Two pupils in front of me quickly wrapped up their gossip.

A red-haired boy behind me did a silent gesture and the rest of the line zipped their lips.

Peter stood tiptoe, looking for me.

My tall figure stood tall like a flamingo at the back of the line.

A moment later, everyone in all grades formed a neat matrix.

It was nighttime.

The silvery moon hung high in the cloudless sky.

A sea of stars was twinkling above our heads.

In the corner of my eyes, I saw a man in an astronaut suit standing below the stage.

He definitely looked creepy.

On his shoulder was the symbol of an American flag.

"Welcome everybody. First, I would like to welcome our distinguished guest from the embassy of Onu II ambassador, Dr. Kim Song Ku. Dr. Kim is a Korean astronaut with Korean aerospace research institute. Two years ago, Dr. Kim was launched into space on TMA 600 and returned to Earth a few months ago. Since returning, she has been working as a senior researcher, as well as a senior space ambassador. Let us welcome Dr. Kim," Miss O' Connor introduced.

"Thank you for giving this precious opportunity for me to talk with you. Thank you for St George Orphan School for inviting me here. I guess many of your have heard of Russia and NASA space program. If you have, please put up your hand," Dr. Kim asked.

Everyone threw their hands up excitedly.

"Very good. Everyone here has heard of them. They have a very long history of the space program. As their sister company, we have secured a contract with them to reserve ten tickets exclusively for St. George Orphan School to go on a space mission. This maybe an exciting and life changing opportunity for you. Any questions?" Dr. Kim advised.

The crowd began to get excited.

"Dr. Kim, why did you decide to go to space?" Peter raised his hand up and asked.

"Earth is becoming too small for us. In the last 200 years, human population has been growing exponentially. This exponential grow cannot continue for the future generation. Uncontrolled population growth also means unsustainable amount of energy consumption. Earth is at an ever-increasing risk of being wiped out by natural disaster. We are running out of space on Earth. We have less than 1000 years on this planet. That is why the future of the human race is space. That is why space exploration is the future of humanity," Dr. Kim explained.

"What is the objective of the space mission?" I asked.

"Two years ago, a wormhole appeared. Jupiter had opened up a path to a distant galaxy with twelve potentially habitable planets. We have colonized the moon of one of the planets, called Zeptune. It is thirty-nine light-years away from Earth. Already, there are human colonists settled there. Your mission is simply to go there and help the colonists to terraform it," Dr. Kim continued.

"How long are we going there?" Tommy threw his hand up to ask.

"Well, this is a very good question. May I ask how old are you?" Dr. Kim questioned.

"I am twelve. Why is that?" Tommy pursued.

"Well, by the time you come back to Earth, you will be celebrating your eighteenth birthday," Dr. Kim said.

W ould you go to space if there was a chance you could never come back to Earth?

Peter and I stared at the cloudless sky in bed all night, thinking.

We are orphans.

And we both love the universe.

Going to space is our dream.

Besides, we don't have any important reasons to be on Earth right now.

Nature, like rain, trees, beaches, oceans, rain and snow, they are probably the most absent things I will miss if I were to go to space.

I won't miss people too much.

After all, my parents are up there, somewhere in space.

So, there is not much I will leave behind.

I love space.

There is no debate.

This is a simple decision.

It is not like I don't like it on Earth.

I like to travel to different place to see different things.

Going to another planet and having a mission to work for a greater cause is pretty exciting.

Perhaps this was why my parents left me behind.

After all, we only live once.

Why not go for a very life changing experience?

Zirgin Galactic headquarters is a vertically assembled building with fifty-two stories.

Embossed on the building is the round logo of Zirgin Galactic on the right and an American flag on the left.

According to Dr. Kim, Zirgin Galactic headquarters is one of the largest single-story building in the world. It is designed to assemble large space vehicles and space shuttles.

And today, it is eye opening for me as I have been selected to go to space.

Our yellow bus threw a turn in a roundabout.

My knees were wobbling and my hands unsteady.

On our left, we saw a space shuttle being rolled into the gaping doorway of the Zirgin Galactic headquarter by a transporter.

"Her name is *Endeavour*. She is both the brain and the heart of our space transportation system. She will be stacked with an external tank, with solid rocket boosters atop the mobile launcher platform for her launch on space exploratory missions," Dr. Kim explained.

"That is so cool." Peter tilted his glasses.

Behind us, Tommy popped his purplish bubblegum bubble.

The laughing, teasing and yelling at the back settled in complete silence.

Everyone was fascinated.

To be honest, this is my first time to see a space shuttle this close.

The bus lurched on.

It exited the roundabout and drove past a few parking lots and blocks of buildings.

Passing green became a hazy blur.

The windows shook with every small bump in the ragged pavement.

Everyone jostled back and forth.

Tommy shifted seats with his mates and slid into a window seat from behind us.

"Hey Peter, why you are going to space?" Tommy slugged Peter hard on the shoulder.

"Because I want to have some space," Peter replied.

Tommy wanted to speak, but he made a gulp sound.

"You made me swallow my gum, Peter."

Everyone behind laughed.

I turned around to see my friend Molly right behind us. She and my other friend Karen were teasing each other with jokes.

Molly and Karen looked much alike. They both have long, wavy brown hair and round, blue eyes. They both are a couple of inches shorter than me. They only real difference is that Molly has a Korean accent.

Sitting in front of them was Sol. He is Tommy's best

pal. Like Tommy, he is a troublemaker who loves to crack jokes to make us laugh all the time.

"So, what is a spaceman's favorite chocolate?" Sol asked.

"Mars bar," Peter answered.

"That is a good one, Peter," Karen was pleased.

"Sol, give us another one," Tommy demanded.

"Why did the cow go to outer space?" Sol asked.

Molly frowned and rephrased his question in her Korean tone.

"To visit the milky way." Peter smiled.

See what I mean.

The shriek of burning fuel drew our attention to the right.

The sound was so powerful that I could feel the whole bus trembling.

A voice was broadcasting a count down from ten to zero.

"What …what was that?"

The bus slowed down.

When we peered through the window, a magnificent view of a space shuttle launch came into sight.

We saw a space shuttle vertically mounted on a tall and red tinted launch pad.

Attached to the space shuttle was a solid rocket booster.

"You guys are lucky to see *Challenger II* launch today." Dr. Kim smiled.

3

Long orange flames spout out from below the rocket like a dragon.

2

Challenger II rose vertically at a ninety-degree angle along the launch pad.

The engine bellowed.

Mushroom-like smoke, grit and dust blanketed the surrounding area at the blink of an eye.

1

And it lifted off.

Everyone clapped as we saw the shuttle rise high above the sky, leaving behind a long trail of orange flame and black smoke.

Higher and higher it raised. Its projectile became parabolic.

Then the shuttle became tinier and tinier until it disappeared from sight.

Rocket booster separation confirmed and guidance now converging.

I always dreamed of seeing a space shuttle launch in person, but I never thought I would see one in person today.

"Dr. Kim, where are they heading?" I asked.

"Challenger II will be going to Interstellar cruiser to register to Zirgin Galactic first. Then they will be assigned to commence an operation to terraform the moon of Zeptune, much like your mission," Dr. Kim replied.

"Can't wait." Tommy popped another bubblegum bubble.

"Oh, you do not need to envy them. Your crew will

be joining them tomorrow evening." Dr. Kim threw us a hideous smile that made me feel uneasy.

***

The brakes squeaked.

Everyone lurched forward as the bus came to a stop.

The exhaust pipe exhaled the last puff of black smoke.

It had been a long ride.

Everyone squeezed through the aisle as we were piling out of the bus.

"Hey Tommy, stop pushing," Peter complained as Tommy bypassed him.

"Leave him alone. Why do you always have to pick on someone two years younger than you?" I challenged.

"Yes. Pick someone of your own size." Peter stuck his tongue out.

"Fine, lady first," Tommy mocked.

As soon as we got off the bus, we saw a block of glass-windowed building, with the company logo, towering above us. The wall beside the entrance was embossed with the metallic words – THE SKY CALLS TO US.

"All right, everyone. This will be your accommodation for tonight – your final night on Earth. Find your keys at the reception area. Enjoy and prepare. I will be seeing all of you inside *Endeavour* tomorrow evening." Dr. Kim waved us a farewell.

The sky darkened.

A swirl of pink and lavender transfigured the sky, making it sad but beautiful.

All of a sudden, I had a mixture of emotions.

Mom. Dad. Where are you up there?

"Hey Nova, what are you up to?"

A voice from nowhere interrupted my thought.

It was Molly and Karen.

"Are you okay?"

"Ya. But knowing this is my last day on Earth makes me feel I am not ready." I exhaled.

"Neither of us are ready," Molly replied, motioning to the rest of the crowd.

"We are all doing this for a cause. Earth is overpopulated, and we need to find and create our new home," Karen said.

"I guess you are right," I replied.

T he automatic door of the glass-windowed building slid open.

Shaft of bright light blinded us.

The next thing we saw was a high ceiling lobby with white walls and bright light that chased away the dimmest shadow.

Hundred of pupils of different nationalities gathered together.

Americans. Chinese. Indians. You name it.

Everyone suited up in white apparel with the company logo embossed on the shoulder.

Everyone was busy socializing with one another.

Interestingly, most of them looked about our age.

"The Apollo moon landing was faked," one of the pupils with a Russian accent challenged. "The whole Apollo program was staged. It is all a hoax."

"Why do you say so?" An American pupil defended.

"If you keep a hawk eye on the space landing footage, there were no stars. Flags were moving by slight breeze. The whole idea of the Apollo mission was merely a competition between U.S. and the Soviet Union. The whole space landing was actually filmed within a large Hollywood studio, with the production funded by Walt Disney," the Russian guy continued.

Everyone's attention was on space conspiracy theories and the unknowns of space.

"Your group must be from St. George Orphan School." A booming voice from behind made the six of us jumped.

When we turned around and saw a little man in a formal suit and bow tie behind us.

The man was at most three-foot seven inches.

His short stature reminded me of dwarfism.

"Yes. We are," I responded.

"Let me introduce myself. My name is Grum. Every-one here calls me Grumpy," Grumpy introduced himself.

"Maybe he should changed his name to Dopey," Tom-my giggled next to Sol.

They burst out laughing.

"Excuse me." Grumpy narrowed his eyes, focusing on the two troublemakers.

"Hey boys, have some manners." I gave them a sharp gaze and turned back to Grumpy. "I apologize for their misbehavior. My name is Nova. Dr. Kim asked us to collect our keys from the reception."

Grumpy gestured us to follow him.

He handed over the keys to our room and advised us to take the elevator.

"Enjoy your last day."

***

That evening, I had a hot shower before suiting up to join others for dinner.

The sensation of the steamy water always calmed me. It always takes my mind off things.

Do you feel the same?

I wonder if I will have the same luxury of a hot water shower in outer space.

Probably not.

I once watched a YouTube video of an Italian space-woman demonstrating how to shower in space. Water in space behaves very differently compared to Earth. I remember how the weightless water stuck to her skin. The spacewoman explains the phenomenon is because of surface tension.

God knows what surface tension is.

Dinnertime finally came.

But, the food really made me arch an eyebrow.

I thought it was going to be one big dinner farewell us to space.

I was dead wrong.

Instead of having something sensational, we had creamed spinach, crackers, shortbread cookies and candy coated peanuts served in a tray.

Are they supposed to be an entree or snacks?

None of them is my favorite.

The cooks told us that we better get used to it because these will be what we will be eating on a routine day.

After dinner, everyone said they want an early sleep.

Well, I can't blame them.

It has been a long day for everyone.

Everyone is exhausted.

I walked outside the glass-windowed building and looked at the star filled sky.

It was beautiful.

I laid down on the slope of the grassland and stared at the stars.

Crickets chirped in proximity.

I remember Dad and I once got lost in the woods without a compass. He told me whenever I get lost in the woods, try to look for Polaris to find the way.

"Dad, why Polaris?" I asked curiously.

"Polaris is the only star that remains almost stationary no matter how much the surrounding changes. It is always there."

"Dad, will you be my Polaris?"

"Silly girl, of course I will always be there for you no matter how much the future changes. I am always your Polaris."

Dad's words play back in my mind, like an old cassette tape.

Dad. Mom, why did you leave me like this?

I focused on Polaris and asked why.

7

I couldn't sleep that night.

I was tossing back and forth in this foreign bed.

Twisting, turning from side to side like an earthworm.

At last, I gave up and decided to take a walk in this unfamiliar space building.

Dr. Kim advised us that we are going to have a short assembly in the morning to brief us on our mission objectives.

Then we are going to board *Endeavour*.

I felt ecstatic.

Going to space has always been my dream.

Maybe that is the reason I can't sleep.

Nova, what happened to you? Oh well, maybe a little walk can help to make me sleep.

So, I decided to exit my room and hurtled down the white, empty corridor to explore this place.

I wanted to wake Peter to tag along with me.

But, he is a sound sleeper. So, I decided to go alone.

I walked and walked, until I reached the end of the corridor where the elevators were.

Then I stepped into the elevator as the door slide open.

What am I doing? Oh well, it doesn't hurt to explore this place a little bit… as long as I remember which floor my room is on.

The rattle and hum of the elevator ascension sang in my ears.

I randomly exited a floor and walked along a branching corridor.

Next, I saw nurses and doctors in white coats exit and enter rooms.

I guess this floor must be a nursing bay.

The raging sound of an angry conversation in a room to my left drew my attention.

It almost sounded like a fight was about to happen inside.

What is going on?

I rested my head on the nearest door and began to eavesdrop.

***

An angry nurse headed to exit the room after fighting with her patient for an injection.

"How is she?" A visitor in brown suit walked in just as the nurse was about to exit. He was holding a briefcase with one hand and a coffee mug with another.

"Terrible." The nurse forced a smile and headed for the exit.

"Hello, my name is Kurt, John Kurt. The company sent me here to see how you are feeling today," Kurt asked softly as he sat beside Eva, who had her back facing him while lying on a hospital bed.

Eva ignored him. She wanted him to leave her alone.

"Okay. I am sorry about what happened to you. But, you just had an unusually long hypersleep. In fact, you are lucky to be alive. It is blind luck that our deep salvage team found you. Otherwise, you could be drifting in space until eternity," Kurt explained.

"What do you mean? How long was I out there?" Eva turned to Kurt.

Their eyes met.

Kurt suddenly felt uncomfortable.

"Has no one discussed with you yet?" Kurt frowned.

"No. I do not recognize this place. Not at all."

Eva looked around. Puzzled.

"Ahh… Okay. You are back on Earth. This is Zirgin Galactic headquarters," Kurt said.

Great. I am back at Earth. I am dying to see my daughter again. Eva thought.

"It is just that this news might shock you." Kurt's voice sounded uneasy.

"What is it? How long?" Eva demanded.

"It is longer than - ," Kurt swallowed hard.

Something isn't right.

"Tell me," Eva pursued. "Please."

"Eighty years."

Reality crashed in.

There is a moment of grief and silence.

Eva was stunned.

This is impossible. She promised her daughter to come back for her birthday. She promised her she would be just gone for a while… until her crew received a distress call on their way home…and the company forced them to investigate… and…

"This isn't real. This isn't happening. Venus." Eva began to cry.

"Here." Kurt handed Eva a vintage photo of an old woman. Her smile looked somehow familiar to Eva, except with wrinkles spread all over her face.

Eva looked at the photo. Her hands were trembling.

"This is your daughter," Kurt spoke. "Died at the age of seventy six. Married. Divorced. No children. Her final wish is to see her mother one day."

"What day is this?" Eva wiped her tears and asked.

"It is the second week of May. It is mother's day," Kurt replied.

He handed Eva all the letters Venus wrote to her every Mother's Day.

Mom. I came first in class. I want to show you the award Mrs. O'Donnell gave me in front of the whole class. Where are you?

Mom. I am picking which university to go to. Can you give me some advice?

Mom. Today is my graduation day. Everyone is taking photos with their parents. Where are you?

Mom. I feel so sad. Leon left me. Where are you?

Eva's shoulder heaved. She missed everything that happened in her daughter's life. Water welled in her eyes again.

The muscle of her chin trembled.

Moment by moment, salty drops ran down her cheeks from her luminous eyes.

"What year am I in now?" Eva asked.

"2150."

The mammoth body of *Endeavour* towered over us in the evening breeze.

Damp evening dew blanketed the grassland where I sat last night.

One by one, we boarded the shuttle in our clumsy suits.

At the entrance of the shuttle, I looked back to have a final glance at the silhouette of the sunrise.

The orange hue rays brought warmth for the day.

The trees shone as if they were wearing golden crowns.

It was alive. It was beautiful.

"Look a rainbow!" Peter exclaimed and pointed his finger to the far north in infinity.

"I guess nature comes and say goodbye." Molly looked deep in thought as she peered out at the rainbow.

"We are missing you already."

The six of us followed a space officer inside the space shuttle.

The air was full of electric buzz and the sounds of machines.

We passed a room, and an engineer was busy tuning knobs and flicking switches of complex machines.

Beside him, another engineer was communicating with the control tower to synchronize the machines.

"Welcome on board, young astronauts." The engineers waved at us. His smile was genuine.

"Good morning." We smiled back.

The six of us walked along a corridor.

The shuffle of our footsteps thundered on the latex floor.

The space officer stopped when we reached the end of the corridor.

He pushed the red button on our left, and the hatch leading to the next room sprang open.

"Dr. Kim is waiting for you in the briefing center," the space officer replied and motioned us in.

I looked over to Tommy and Sol.

Their giggles echoed down the corridors from behind.

Tommy smacked Sol on the chest. And Sol pushed him back.

They were behaving like silly kids.

"They are so embarrassing." Karen shook her head.

Molly, Peter and I nodded and agreed.

The interior of the briefing center was an oversized compartment with a multi user hologram table in the middle. There were four doors in each room that led to different areas of the shuttle.

"Morning, my students from St. George Orphan School. Welcome on board. In a couple of hours, *Endeavour* will liftoff. You will be suited up with an entry suit.

Your first destination will be Interstellar cruiser ST-132. Your work here is important. It is the future of the human race – to terraform and colonize potential habitable planets. Once you board the cruiser, you will be trained. You will be assigned to travel to a moon called Zeptune," Dr. Kim briefed.

"How many colonists are there in Zeptune?" I asked.

"There are seventy families there. More coming. So, you are not the first to go there. Atmosphere processors were installed. We just need more young people like you to help with terraforming," Dr. Kim answered.

"What is an atmosphere processor?" Peter questioned.

"It is what makes the air breathable in different planets," Dr. Kim replied.

"What do you mean?" Molly asked in her Korean accent.

"Before atmospheric processing began, the atmosphere of Zeptune contained high levels of nitrogen, methane and carbon dioxide crystals. The surface was deep cold. So, the function of the atmosphere processors was to make the planet's atmosphere breathable and up to habitable temperature," Dr. Kim elaborated.

"Will we ever run out of air?" Sol joked.

"Do you mean oxygen?" Dr. Kim corrected.

"Yes."

"We never had such incident over thirty years. We have sixty-six atmospheric processors installed around the terraformed colony. Plenty of backups. Besides, we are always communicating with Zeptune. In case there is an emergency, we will always watch your back. You are making history," Dr. Kim confirmed.

***

The six of us sat vertically in a narrow compartment.

The suit technicians checked if everyone was suited.

Technicians from the headquarters and our shuttle were busy confirming everyone was okay over the radio. The background static sound was annoying.

The countdown sang in our ears.

The six of us looked at each other nervously as the shuttle was about to take off.

Chill and excitement crept down our bones.

Sol, the bully, was busy praying to God. Sweat was pouring down his forehead.

It is going to be a long roller coaster ride. I decided.

"Peter, are you all right?" I asked.

Peter saluted in return.

Before I could say another word, *Endeavour* roared loudly, and the momentum glued me to my seat.

My ears began to hurt. Within seconds, I heard nothing. It was as if the whole world was muted.

Howl!

Tommy howled like a werewolf under a full moon.

Higher and higher, *Endeavour* flew vertically in a perfect ninety-degree angle.

Its engine continued to spur orange flames.

Its trail was like a stroke of orange from a clever artist.

In my opinion, it was the state of art with the help of technology.

I tried to look out from the porthole, but everything looked like flying color.

The radio continued to confirm our system and the

fuel cells were in good shape.

The boosters that lifted us into the atmosphere burnt out and detached. Guidance system activated.

Endeavour continued to thrust up.

The sky transited from white to black.

"We have just reached escape velocity," one of the engineers confirmed.

Minutes later, I felt silence and stillness like never before.

When I looked out at the porthole again, I saw something very few people are lucky enough to see in their life.

It is the magnificent Earth view from space.

9

Earth is dying.

The once glorious blue of our planet is slowly turning into a desert landscape.

Many years ago, I remember a famous physicist, Stephen Hawking, once said the long-term future of the human race must be in space.

Global warming, overpopulation, rising water level are killing our planet.

Our seasons shift.

The average temperature of summer is fifty degrees Celsius.

A few years ago, a mega tsunami destroyed many of the major cities around the world.

Venice was devoured by the sea.

Now, either we spread to other planets, or we face extinction.

I read that Mars and Earth were similar 3.5 billion years ago. Water once flowed freely on the Red Planet. But, something happened. Nobody knew where the water went. Some scientists say that the Martian water evaporated into space because the planet's magnetic field collapsed. Others speculate that the water on Mars never left at all. They were absorbed into water bearing mineral rock by some irreversible chemical reaction.

Whatever reason, it is a scary to imagine how Earth is becoming like Mars from the view in space.

Endeavour's voyage continued.

Another rocket boosted.

Earth was becoming smaller and smaller until it disappeared from sight.

Goodbye Earth.

10

I always dreamed about going to space.

I wonder how it feels being weightless.

Here I am, floating in midair in a compartment in *Endeavour*.

My hair was flying everywhere.

It is the wildest thing I have ever done.

It is …it is like nothing I have ever experienced.

If you ask me, I can only say it is like you feel heavier, heavier at first, and then feel lighter and lighter, and eventually just float up.

It is really like flying.

Sometimes, the reference point is the ground.

Other times, we were upside down and our reference became the ceiling.

"Wow. Molly, you are on the ceiling." Karen laughed.

"Oh my god, I have no idea what to say!" Molly screamed joyfully.

See what I mean.

Dr. Kim threw up some colorful candy in midair for us to catch.

The candy floated randomly in space.

Sol, Peter, and Tommy were fighting for them.

"I feel like I am Pac-man," Peter joked.

Everybody laughed.

Dr. Kim said that every object has a sticker on it. She said it is important the objects stick to a surface; otherwise, it will fly off and get lost somewhere else.

We flew behind Dr. Kim as she gave us some training on how to use the space toilet and the kitchen.

Next, Dr. Kim introduced the sleeping chamber. She calls it the small pods. Inside each pod was only a green sleeping bag tied to a wall. Nothing more.

"Is…is this the place we are going to sleep?" Tommy cried in disbelief.

"Yes. Of course," Dr. Kim replied.

"Where are the pillows and mattress?"

"In space, you don't need a pillow or a matrass. There is no gravity. You can just comfortably relax. You don't need pillow to hold your head up. You can just relax every muscle in your body and your arms float up in front of you." Dr. Kim smiled.

She flew off to the end of the corridor and turned right.

"This is where I spend up to eight hours a day here. It is my sleep pod. It is actually on the floor. But, once you are inside, you just can't tell," Dr. Kim continued.

Eight hours until destination.

The A.I. of the shuttle announced.

"Oh well, maybe it is a good idea to get some sleep

before we dock," Dr. Kim suggested.

Everyone agreed.

***

I lost track of time sleeping in space.

It was so quite. So comfortable. So peaceful.

When I woke up and joined the others in a compartment, I saw the mouth of a colossal space station towering above us outside our cockpit.

Endeavour is being swallowed by a space station.

Except in movies, I have never seen this giant space station in my life.

"This is interstellar cruiser ST-132." Dr. Kim admired. "The greatest invention in space history."

The six of us clustered behind her.

Our pilot received a transmission from the control tower of ST-132.

The hum of *Endeavour* turned into a metallic groan as it landed.

The giant airlock of ST-132 closed after we entered.

Then *Endeavour's* door hissed open.

A short ramp slid down from it with a rattle, clunking onto the surface of the giant space station.

All the crewmembers descend the ramp and broad interstellar cruiser ST-132.

Everyone looked excited.

Interesting enough, the effect of zero gravity was gone.

We felt like we were on earth again.

A tall man with gray hair and long face greeted us with his hideous smile. Apparently, there is a scar on his face.

Standing beside him were two tough looking colonial

marines. Armed.

"Welcome back, Dr. Kim. Are these our new recruits?" The tall man wore a smile.

"Of course. They are brave, young volunteers to give up everything to come here." Dr. Kim turned to us.

"Very good. I am impressed. I am General Muesel, the commanding officer of vessel ST-132," General Muesel introduced.

"Sir –" Tommy began to speak but was interrupted by General Muesel with a cough.

"It is General," Dr. Kim whispered to correct him.

"Sorry, General Muesel, what work is involved in terraforming Zeptune?" Tommy continued.

General Muesel motioned us to the Powered work loader - a commercial mechanized exoskeleton for lifting heavy objects and cargoes.

The pilot inside was our age.

"Z-5000 Powered work loader, powered by hydrogen fuel cell up to 65kW of power. The loader arm can hold up to 250kg of concrete each. It is engineered to multiply human operator's strength several thousand times. You will be using these to terraform Zeptune," General Muesel explained.

Molly and Karen swallowed hard.

"Don't worry. I am just kidding. You won't be doing those yet." General Muesel smirked.

"So…what will we be doing?" Karen stammered.

There is a moment of silence.

All of a sudden, I have an uneasy feeling.

That smirk of the General gave me creeps.

"Right now, you will only have one job. And that is to

settle down. It is a long ride here from Earth," General Muesel spoke.

We followed General Muesel as he showed us around the interior of ST-132.

Marines saluted the General as we walked by.

"Zirgin Galactic is an America Japanese company founded by the merger of Zirgin corp and Galactic corp. The company is primarily a technology supplier, manufacturing synthetics, spaceships, computers and is now a frontier of interplanetary shipping and transport. One of our corporate interests now is to operate human colonies." General Muesel walked us to the upper level and passed a meeting room.

I looked inside the meeting room.

At the corner of my eyes, I saw an angry woman shouting. She looked frustrated.

Hang on a second. That woman looked familiar.

"Did my IQ just drop sharply while I was away?" the woman asked. "Ma'am, I already said it was not indigenous."

The rest of the faces in the meeting room looked at each other.

Some of them were humoring her. Some looked in disbelief. The rest looked embarrassed even to be there.

"But, Officer Eva, the analysis team went over the complex centimeter by centimeter and found no evidence of that thing you described," an old woman in the bio division reported.

"There have been colonists living in ED-209 for almost a decade. The military received no complains from them about it," a lieutenant with five stars on his shoulder added.

I turned my head to stare back at the woman as I walked.

Suddenly, General Muesel's deep voice interrupted my thoughts.

"Are you okay?" General Muesel asked.

"Oh. It is nothing. Who is this woman?" I asked curiously.

"This woman is sick. She is mentally unstable," General Muesel said.

"But why?" I pursued.

"We are charging her for blowing up a M-class star freighter that costs fifty million dollars in adjusted dollar and killing everyone onboard." General Muesel smirked. "We are suspending her ICC license indefinitely as commercial flight officer and filing criminal charges against her," General Muesel explained.

"Why would she do that?" I was confused.

"For unknown reasons," General Muesel replied. "Now, would you finally like to follow us?"

I gaze at that woman one more time and hurry to catch up with the others.

We arrived at a stairwell and a big square LED, showing Level 3, illuminating our way.

"Dr. Kim, do you know why we can walk like we were on Earth in here?" Peter was puzzled.

"ST-132 has an artificial gravity generator," Dr. Kim replied.

"Artificial gravity?" Peter frowned.

"ST-132 is spinning to stimulate Earth's gravity, but you don't feel it." Dr. Kim forced a smile.

I gazed around. I can hardly believe the whole cruiser is spinning at all.

Or is it?

We kept moving.

A short while later, we arrived at a wide, hexagonal corridor.

Bright white light strips on the floor and wall illuminated our path.

On both sides of the corridor were rows of rooms that extended all the way to the end of the corridor.

Everything looked clean and tidy.

"These will be your compartments. You will be staying in here for now. Dr. Kim will introduce you to the crewmembers tomorrow. You will be trained. And you will be ready for our mission. Are there any questions?" General Muesel asked.

We shook our head.

"Dismissed."

PART 2

11

We spent the next couple of months in ST-132 receiving different trainings.

In our spare time, we explore the interstellar cruiser.

Believe it or not, this place is enormous.

There are shopping malls, gyms and video game centers.

Everything you need on Earth is here.

The General told us that everyone transacts with interplanetary-cryptocurrency, known as the P-coin. He said that no one deals with cash nowadays. Cash is only for the ones who don't like a deep business record.

Well, you may wonder how we earn P-coin income.

Actually, it is pretty simple.

All we have to do is to create value .

Let's say, for example, we can help to plant. We can help to generate heat and electricity. We can help to make water. We can build or service atmospheric processing plant to convert unbreathable air into one that is suitable for human habitation. It can be anything that creates value to help the company colonize other planets.

To me, it is way more practical.

It sure beats doing algebra in class.

Also, everyone has the chance to specialize in something.

For me, I picked a major in fixing the atmospheric processing plant. I picked that because it is the foundation of terraforming on any planet.

Peter picked his favorite discipline – mechanics.

Tommy and Sol picked to join the colonial marines since they like guns.

Molly has chosen to learn about computers and artificial intelligence.

For Karen, well, she was undecided for the first few weeks, but finally choose planting. I know it is boring. But, it is also crucial to know how to grow food on spacecraft and on other planets for sustainable deep space missions.

One day, we finally received a direct order from General Muesel to commence our first mission - Terraform Zeptune.

Our new ship is called Soduku – a light cruiser piloted by an AI called Okaa-san.

I meet a Japanese crewmember called Hiroyuki from Challenger II.

He was twelve. He has narrow eyes and black hair like a typical Asian. Unlike us, he is formal but shy. He told me that he is from Tokyo.

He laughed when I told him that I saw his shuttle liftoff that day.

When I asked him why he decided to go to space, he said that Japan is constantly threatened by natural disasters. In the not too distant future, massive volcanic eruption might make the country extinct. That is why he joined Zirgin Galactic to go to space as a Japanese.

"Team, Zeptune has an equatorial diameter of 12,000km. It has a surface gravity of 0.7 to that of Earth. A large scale of terraforming and human colonization began two years ago. A number of atmosphere processing plants are already in place," Dr. Kim briefed.

"How long is our flight?" I asked.

"Zeptune is only thirty-nine light years away." Dr. Kim sounded uneasy.

Everyone dropped their mouth open, except Peter.

"By the time we arrive, we will be in our thirties," Tommy complained.

"Light years is the unit of distance, not time," Peter corrected.

"I am just testing if you are listening," Tommy said.

"Soduku is capable to travel very close to the speed of light. When you come back to Earth, you will just be graduating high school," Dr. Kim corrected.

"How is that possible?" Sol was confused.

"Time dilation." Dr. Kim wore a thin smile. "By the time you return to Earth, it will be a very different place. Let's just say… you time travel."

"Very funny," Tommy cried in disbelief.

"Do I look like I am joking?" Dr. Kim tilted her glasses and said.

12

The hypersleep chamber is a tube-like capsule.

According to Dr. Kim, the chamber has something call the stasis field. Any materials or living beings that fall under the umbrella of the field can survive for thousands or millions of years beyond their normal lifetimes.

It is a 22nd century long space travel technology that allows humans to survive very long trips in space.

The good news is that we will be in hypersleep state most of the time during our voyage.

It will be the longest sleep I have ever had in my life.

Isn't that amazing?

The glass door of the hypersleep chamber opened up like flower petals.

After our final meal, I said goodnight to my crew.

Then I slid in the capsule.

To my surprise, the capsule was more spacious than I thought.

When I looked closer, the glass of each hypersleep chamber is equipped with a holographic display that communicates with Okaa-san – the ship's AI.

Okaa-san can monitor everyone's metabolic conditions.

I swipe the screen of the capsule to select my favorite music.

Unfortunately, it did not help to put me into sleep.

I changed the channel to some space relaxing music.

Now, that's better.

The looping soundtrack was meditating, at the same time, hypnotizing.

My mind kept thinking about the strange woman shouting in the meeting room.

The image of Mom and Dad celebrating my birthday flashed in my head.

Their voice is soothing.

It is as if they are right next to me.

Soon, the hyper sleep pods were coated in a layer of frost.

Whiter and whiter.

My mind caught in a carousel of thoughts.

My eyes felt heavier and heavier.

I was drifting into sleep.

13

I had a dream.

I had a long dream.

I dreamt of myself on a bridge surrounded by fog and mist.

Everything else was engulfed by darkness.

My heart was pounding, mind empty.

From a distance, I could see two figures ahead of me.

They looked familiar.

I raced after them.

I recognized their back.

Mom? Dad? I cried.

They returned their head to look at me for a second.

Their faces were expressionless.

Pale and cold.

They ignored me and continued on their way.

Mom? Dad?

Don't leave me.

I don't want to be alone.

The feeling of despair, desperate and anguish enveloped my heart.

I chased after them with all my strength.

But I couldn't keep up with them.

Mom. Dad. Wait!

How can you abandon me like this?

How could -

Before I could finish, I lost my balance and stumbled into a hole on the bridge.

Down and down I fell into the bottomless pit.

Down and down I fell into the abyss.

My hope of seeing Mom and Dad was swallowed by despair.

Then I was awakened by the sound of my own breathing.

My forehead was sweating.

My whole body was numb.

My hands clutched to my chest. I felt rapid, fluttered movement of the beating of my heart.

Nightmares.

An ominous feeling haunted me.

I had this dream multiple times when I was four.

The nightmare carries on.

Why am I having this dream again?

The holographic display on the window in front of me flickered into life.

It had some transition and became an overhead med-monitor.

I punched a few buttons.

Then the retractable fiberglass frame of the hyper-sleep chamber lifted open.

I slowly sat up and stretched.

The fluorescent light tube in the cylindrical room flickered momentarily before it lit.

Everyone was still sleeping soundly.

I lifted my feet out of the chamber into the freezing floor.

"Cold. Cold."

My feet danced around the floor until I managed to suit up in a space costume.

The dome surveillance camera at the corner was watching me.

I hate being monitored.

Where is my privacy?

I exited the hypersleep chamber.

Then I found myself in a hexagonal corridor in zero gravity again.

I swam like a dolphin in water.

The entire vessel was still and silent, except for the constant electric buzz and the sound of computers.

I looked around.

Several monitors were evenly spaced below the chamber of the ceiling. They were displaying infographics and spectrums in neon and green.

I exited the corridor through a hexagonal slid door.

I continued to swim through the next corridor and took the one that branched off to the main hallway.

The sound of an advertisement faded in.

Zirgin Galactic offers a better alternative. A better way of life. There is no colony more beautiful than Zeptune – the jewel of space colonization.

The holographic representation of a smiling woman was presenting the destination we will be in. It showed an amazing place with fancy dome shaped buildings plated with solar cells. Plants grow along the highway. Vehicles were flying to and from buildings.

I don't believe in these propagandas.

I wonder what Zeptune really looks like.

The hallway of Soduku was a gigantic three-story shopping hall.

The wall was a giant floor to ceiling glass panel showing a sensational space background with the beautiful curve of Earth.

Earth. It was so near and yet so far…

I wandered around different shops in different levels.

Cosmetic shops. Hairdressing shops. Clothing shops. Cinemas. Restaurants.

Everything was run by artificial intelligence.

Everything was transacted with P-coins.

Everything was automated.

A while later, my stomach began to growl.

So, I went inside a restaurant called the Robot Kitchen and ordered my first space lasagna with a tablet.

There was no chef but only a pair of fully articulated robotic arms integrated on a beautiful, professional looking kitchen.

When the robotic hand cooked, it looked like it was replaying the exact movement of a master chef!

When I studied the manual carefully, I discovered I can even pick the cooking style of different famous chefs.

Amazing!

Hum. Maybe I will try something else tomorrow.

After my meal, I wandered around for a couple more

hours.

A few cleaning robots in disk shape were busy crawling on the ground despite zero gravity.

The entire hallway was empty and hollow but clean.

It looks like I am the only one in here.

Where is everyone?

I swam back to the first floor where there was a station that has the letter *i* on it.

It must be the information desk I decided.

"Hello, where is everyone?" I asked.

"Hello Nova, we are on Sudoku," The robot answered.

Nova? It knows my name?

"I need to talk to a person," I requested.

"What sort of person? Personal assistant? Personal loans? Personal interest?"

"Hey, wait, slow down," I said. "I need to speak with Dr. Kim."

"Dr. Kim is not onboard," the robot said.

"Huh? Then who is our supervisor? Who should I talk to?" I pursued.

"You should talk to the captain that handles passenger's affairs. It is on level three of the grand concourse," the robot responded.

"Thanks."

"Happy to help."

I swam all the way to the third level.

I wonder who is the captain that the robot is taking about?

I followed the road map and ventured past one corridor after another.

Eventually, I arrived in a dome shaped room that had

a brass plate engraved with the words captain Okaa-san outside the door. In the center of the room was a crystal ball like object that radiates different color.

Okaa-san? Isn't this the ship's core AI?

Haven't I requested to talk to a person instead?

"Hello Nova, I am Okaa-san, the captain of the ship. You shouldn't be here."

A digital female voice from nowhere made me jump.

"Okaa-san, am I the only one awake?" I asked the void.

"Yes."

"When will we arrive at Zeptune?" I wondered.

"Suduko has just travelled two light years. We will arrive in Zeptune in approximately twenty-one years," Okaa-san replied.

"What do you mean?" I dropped my mouth open.

"We will arrive in Zeptune in twenty-one years, two months, two weeks, one day, seven hours and fifty-five minutes travelling at ninety percent at the speed of light," Okaa-san clarified.

"So… I still need to wait for another twenty-one years, two months in this spaceship to get to Zeptune? I will be old by the time I get there," I almost choked out.

"Cryogenic suspension during Hypersleep suspends and slows down biological metabolism significantly. The point of stasis is to slow down aging. By the time you arrive in Zeptune, your biological age is significantly lower than your chronological age. You must return back to hypersleep at once," Okaa-san advised. "But –"

"But, what?"

"Putting a person into hibernation requires special

equipment and procedures. The chambers are designed to keep you into hibernation and wake you up at the right time."

14

I was stunned.

Does that means I will be by myself for the rest of my life?

I have always been alone.

But, not like this.

Even without my biological parents, St. George Orphan School adopted me since I was an orphan. Miss O' Connor was like my second mother. I had friends. I could share my feelings with others. I felt love. I had a life.

Right now, I felt cold and empty.

Loneliness is my only friend.

It feasts on my soul like paradise.

In space, there is neither morning nor night.

No oceans. No wind.

No squirrels wake me up in the morning.

No crickets disturb me at night.

Even gravity deserted me.

No one will talk to me ever again, except those stupid AI.

Silence sang in my ears.

I kept imagining the same thing over and over again everyday, with no one to talk to.

No way will I spend the rest of my life like this.

I will go mad!

One of my main purposes of going to space is that…I have a slim chance of seeing my parents again. I know it may sound stupid. But, there is chance.

I must go back into hibernation mode.

***

I spent the next few days studying the hypersleep chamber technical manual.

To be honest with you, it is beyond my comprehension.

It is like…rocket science to me.

The instruction on the manual made me feel like I have dyslexia.

While I was reading, the characters on the manual seemed to dance on the page…mocking my stupidity of going to space.

Then I slowly drifted into sleep.

Day after day, I kept doing the same thing over and over again.

Eat. Sleep. Explore.

I tried almost every single menu in the Robot Kitchen.

Why am I the only one awake?

Hello! Can someone please talk to me?

Back on Earth, I always wish to have some space.

Now, I have it all.

People always tell me to be careful what I wish for,

because one day it will come true.

I decided to swim to the captain room again to complain.

"Hello, this is Okaa-san from Zirgin Galactic. How can I be your service?"

"Okaa-san, why am I the only one awake?" I complained.

Okaa-san didn't reply.

"Respond. I want to write an email back to Earth. This malfunction is ridiculously," I screamed.

"No problem. Your complaint email will arrive in Zirgin Galactic HQ in eleven years. Earliest reply is twenty-one years," Okaa-san replied.

"Tw…twenty years?" I arched my eyebrows in disbelief.

I dropped to my knees.

My emotions swirled like ocean current.

"Why me?" I yowled to myself.

Before I could say another word, my voice was muffled by an interrupting transmission.

"What is going on?" I asked, looking around.

Puzzled.

Okaa-san remained silent.

She was busy tracing the origin of the transmission.

I hurried to the screens in front of me.

One of the screens was showing our ship had intercepted a transmission of an unknown origin.

Another screen was showing other crewmembers in the hypersleep chamber slowly waking up.

I could see Tommy was yawning.

Peter was wrapping his hands around his shoulders.

Molly and Karen looked puzzled.

"Wow…wow…Okaa-san, hang on a second. Why are you waking everyone up?" I cried in horror, knowing they can't be put back into hypersleep.

"My protocol is preset that any transmission indicating a possible emergency SOS signal or intelligent origin must be investigated," Okaa-san explained.

"Who is broadcasting this potential SOS signal?" I arched my eyebrows.

Okaa-san did not reply.

I concentrated on studying the transmission.

But it was too noisy, so I could not make anything meaningful out of it.

"Decoding transmission," Okaa-san announced.

A SOS signal in the middle of space?

I wonder what kind of emergency it is.

I wonder who that can possibly be.

Whoever that might be, the person should thank God that Sudoku found the signal.

It is one in a million in probability.

"The transmission is a distress signal broadcast from a planet orbiting a black hole calls Fornax A," Okaa-san said.

"So, what do you suggest we do?" I asked.

"Like me, your contract with Zirgin Galactic says any systematized transmission indicating a possible intelligent origin must be investigated," Okaa-san said.

"No. This is your contract. Not mine. Besides, I don't remember signing any contract," I said.

"You have authorized Dr. Kim to sign it on your behalf. After all, she is your guidance," Okaa-san explained.

"No way Dr. Kim would have done something like that. We are supposed to terraform Zeptune. This is why I am here. I think there is a mistake somewhere," I argued.

Suddenly, a voice from nowhere interrupted us.

The transmission has been successfully decoded.

"Th….this is…..Dr. Cool. If you…are listening to this … turn back…stay away from…ED209. I repeat. Stay away."

Then the transmission was cut sharp by static noises.

Silence dominated the room once again.

Dr. Cool? I wonder who is he? Why he is broadcasting a SOS signal warning us to turn our ship away.

15

"Is this some kind of joke? Are you trying to force us to go down there to rescue him?" Tommy cried.

"What if we don't comply?" Molly asked.

"Soduku will remain stationary in space until the rescue mission is accomplished," Okaa-san repeated.

"This is ridiculous. We are not signed up for any rescue mission. I want to talk to Dr. Kim." Karen rolled her eyes.

"Dr. Kim is not onboard," I revealed.

Everyone looked at me in disbelief.

"Then who is our supervisor?" Sol asked.

"I am."

A booming voice from behind the crowd drew our attention.

It was a woman in her mid-thirties.

She was tall with curly hair - a typical motherly figure.

Somehow, she looked very familiar.

I have seen her somewhere before…

"My name is Eva. I am your supervisor from now on," Eva said.

"Can you please explain to me what is going on? We are supposed to head to Zeptune. Going down there will delay our mission," Hiroyuki challenged in his Japanese accent.

"Hiroyuki San, have you heard the transmission yourself? We have a SOS emergency signal not far from us. It is a human life we are dealing with. We must form a troop and head down there," Eva said, with arms akimbo. "Now, who are the volunteers to go down with me?"

No one dared to raise their hands.

Since Sol, Tommy and I were among the eldest, we had no choice but to volunteer.

"But the signal is coming from a planet orbiting black hole Fornax A," Peter reminded. He shook his head as if it is a bad idea.

"What are you implying, dude?" Tommy asked.

"Albert Einstein once says that in his theory of relativity that clocks run slower when they are closer to the source of gravity. Fornax A is a super massive black hole not even light can escape. Traveling to a planet this close to the black hole will have dramatic effect on time," Peter explained.

"So?" Tommy frowned.

"So our spaceship is essentially travelling through space as well as time." Peter sounded excited, "If we travel to a planet this close to a black hole, we are travelling in a natural time machine."

"Whatever. Too difficult for me," Tommy said.

"Okaa-san, Bring up the planet," Eva commanded.

The hologram table in the middle of the room sprang to life.

A circular green time-space grid was projected above it.

At the center was Fornax A – an elliptical supermassive black hole that is slowly swallowing nearby planets.

Orbiting around Fornax A were three planets.

The closest one is called Wiur - a blue ocean planet.

"Captain Eva, we have located Dr. Cool's signal," Okaa-san confirmed.

A tiny red dot appeared on Wiur to pinpoint the location.

"Okaa-san , prepare a dropship. Come on, boys and girls. We are moving out."

16

Eva threw a few switches in our drop ship, and the engine ignited.

A strong thrust ejected us from Sudoku.

"Wow!" Tommy and Sol cried with enjoyment.

Peter held his glasses tightly.

I sat back.

Everything vibrated recklessly.

"You are going too fast," I warned.

"Easy. I piloted a M-class star freighter. This is a piece of cake." Eva grinned.

A moment like blackness became gray and white.

We have entered Wiur's atmosphere.

"I can feel the air." Eva took a deep breath.

The engine was whistling.

The ride was bumpy as if we were in some kind of turbulence.

My eyes locked on outside the windows.

It looks like we are flying through clusters of cumulo-nimbus clouds.

Eva continued to accelerate.

A moment later, the cloud scattered.

"It is only ocean!" we exclaimed.

I looked at the endless blue above the sky.

It reminded me of Earth.

"700 meters," Eva announced.

She pulled the pilot stick left and threw everyone to the left.

Everything outside the window turned diagonal.

"Look. A spaceship." Peter motioned us to the gray drop ship crashed landed on the water, floating.

"It must be Dr. Cool's ship," I said.

The vibration continued.

"300 meters," Eva announced and thrust downwards.

I gazed at the gray drop ship a fraction of a second. It disappeared as soon as Eva tilted the craft with a sharp U turn and everyone propelled forward.

When I looked out at the window again, I saw our spacecraft casting a long triangular spray below us, and we landed

"Very graceful," I appraised.

"No. Very rusty." Eva threw me a smile.

17

The back door of our drop ship slowly slid opened.

Shaft of sunlight filtered through the gap of the door, blinding us for a nanosecond.

Next, all of us were bathed in the warmth of the sunlight.

When we reopened our eyes again, an endless turquoise ocean appeared in front of us.

There were no seagulls. No fish.

There was nothing except the sound of the crashing waves.

Everyone stood like a statue at the edge of the drop ship.

This scene is sensational.

We all felt astonished.

No one would have expected a giant ocean like this exists in space.

Eva tested the water and slowly lowered herself into the ocean.

"It is warm," she whispered.

Two marines joined her and dived into the ocean.

"Careful everyone; it is deep," Eva warned.

Sol and Tommy joined Eva, followed by Hiroyuki and me.

Peter did not join us. His legs were shaking.

"Come on, Peter. What you are waiting for?" Tommy mocked.

"Don't tell us you are afraid of water," Sol added.

"Yes, you are right. Peter is suffering from aquaphobia. He almost drowned in a swimming pool when he was five. That is why he gets anxious in front of the ocean," I explained to everyone.

"Such a pussy cat." Tommy shook his head.

"Why does Tommy have to be so mean to Peter?" Hiroyuki whispered next to me.

"Because he is a jerk," I replied.

"Peter, you can stay inside the drop ship," Eva commanded. "The rest of the team, join us to search for Dr. Cool. He should be near. You can use the device on your gauntlet to track him down. Remember, we don't have much time. An hour on Wiur means one Earth year will pass. We cannot afford staying here for too long. An hour at most."

After Eva dismissed us, she and another two marines searched East and West.

Sol and Tommy swam north.

Hiroyuki and I headed south.

I never imagined myself swimming like this in space.

Not in an ocean like this.

I swam steadily under the glittering sunlight.

The wave lapped gently under me.

The water sparkled as if a billion tiny diamonds floated on the surface.

"Did you see anything?" Sol asked over his radio.

"Nothing yet," I replied.

"Forty five minutes left. Keep searching," Eva reminded.

We continued to swim further and further.

Occasionally, I would turn my head to check if Peter is okay by himself.

Poor boy. You should have stay with Molly and Karen. You shouldn't have volunteered to be here.

PING.

My gauntlet signaled me.

Huh?

I lowered my head to glance at the reading.

There is something within our search perimeter.

"Everyone, I have a signal here. The signal is weird. It looks like an interference or something," I broadcasted.

"Look! A dropship!" Hiroyuki exclaimed.

He pointed at the distanced wrecked silvery metal that was submerged into the water.

PING, PING, PING.

The signal grew.

This must be it. I decided.

"We have located a wrecked spacecraft. I repeat. We have located a wrecked spacecraft," I reported.

"Good work. We are coming over," Eva appraised.

PING, PING, PING.

The frequency of the ping grew.

Somehow it gave me an ominous feeling. I had this intuition when I was small. I had sixth sense when something bad was about to happen. Just like the time when my parents left me for the space mission and never returned…

But, what is it this time?

Hiroyuki and I slowed our stroke when we were about to reach the drop ship.

I turned my head and saw the rest of the crew hurrying from behind.

I gazed at the watch.

Thirty minutes. Thirty minutes is all we have to rescue Dr. Cool back to our drop ship.

Just as I was about to begin the rescue myself, Hiroyuki gave me a slight shove in the shoulder and motioned to the far distance.

"Mountains," Hiroyuki frowned.

"Sis…sister…get… back here… now!" Peter screamed on top of his lung over the radio.

I took a few steps towards the mountain.

I listened hard. The sound fainted at first, then it grew louder by the second.

"Hiroyuki San. It…it is not mountain. It…is a wave."

18

"Abort the mission. Everybody get back! Get back to the drop ship! I repeat. Everyone get back to the dropship now!" Eva ordered.

"But, Dr. Cool is just inside," Hiroyuki refused.

He disobeyed the order and hurried to the hatch of the wrenched drop ship.

"Hiroyuki San, what are you doing? There is no time," I tried to grab him.

Unfortunately, I wasn't quick enough. He thrashed away.

The ocean rumbled like an earthquake.

"Oh no…"

When I raised my head again, the wave towered above my head. As tall as a skyscraper!

"We are leaving," Tommy and Sol yelled at us from a distance.

"We are not leaving without Dr. Cool," Hiroyuki insisted.

The huge wave swelled.

It rose higher and higher, like a colossal geyser.

"I got it," Hiroyuki said.

I saw him dragging a fainted old man out of the wrecked drop ship.

But, the old man was too heavy for him.

He struggled and fell.

Without hesitation, I dived towards Hiroyuki to give him a hand.

I know it is suicide.

If I don't help Hiroyuki, he will definitely be swallowed by the wave.

A long shadow casted over us, like a storm.

"What is that?" Hiroyuki asked.

I dared not to reply Hiroyuki. He was unaware.

"Don't ask. Don't look back. Just swim for our life," I cried.

The breeze of the wave was freezing cold.

My whole body chilled as if the temperature was in free fall.

Howling wind sang in my ears.

Rain paddled on my face.

Dark shadow of the wave loomed over us without mercy.

"Oh no," I wailed.

My hope of getting back to my spaceship was swallowed by despair.

"Come on! Come on! You can make it."

Everyone was back on the dropship, except us.

They encouraged us over the radio.

"Sister! Hurry!" Peter shrieked on top of his lung.

The giant wave stretched out too quickly.

My heart was pounding so fast that it almost skipped

a beat.

My body felt exhausted.

Hiroyuki and I choked in one mouthful salty seawater after another as we stroke.

I was breathing hard.

The monster is right behind us, waiting to devour us.

I know I am not going to make it.

The monster is moving way too fast.

It is already too late for us.

The team will have to leave us or else they will be swallowed by the wave too.

I never imagined my journey in space would end this soon.

I am sorry Mom.

I am sorry Dad.

I am sorry…

19

"Go. Go. I am not going to make it. I am not going to make it," I demanded the team breathlessly.

"Yes, you will make it. Yes, you will," Peter cried over the radio.

"Go now. Please," I pleaded.

"We have sent help. Hang in there!" Peter assured.

I felt my body become heavy.

Everything turned blurry.

The wind arose.

It slammed the frenzied drops of water onto our helmet like thousands of tiny stones.

The ocean was turbulent and unforgiving.

The next thing I realized was that I was swimming backwards…

"Hiroyuki San?" I turned around to look at my bubby.

Apparently, he was losing consciousness too.

"I am sorry, Nova. I am so sleepy. So sleepy, I am counting on you to carry the doctor back."

"Hiroyuki San, Wake up! Don't sleep. I can't carry him back by myself. I need you."

The monster wave rose so high that it smothered the sunlight.

Howl, Howl, Howl.

The gale sang in a single tone as it was casting a curse.

Sleep now…you have done enough. Rest in peace.

Just as I was about to give up, a strong pair of arms lifted the three of us up from behind like feathers.

"What the?"

I was stunned.

Before I realized, a strong thrust rocketed us away from the monstrous wave.

Then everything went black.

***

When I reopened my eyes, I was in a brightly lit room.

There was no one else in the room except Eva.

"How are you feeling?" Eva asked. She looked solemn.

"I guess… I am all right."

I tried to sit up, but my muscle ached.

"Take it easy. We are back in Soduku. We almost didn't make it. It was a close one," Eva said.

I was relived but sorry for letting the team down.

"How long have I been sleeping?" I asked.

"Three days," Eva replied.

"How are Hiroyuki San and Dr. Cool?"

"They are okay. They are in the next room."

"I see."

"Why did you disobey my orders?" Eva demanded.

"I…umm…"

"What you were doing was reckless and stupid. You could have gotten yourself killed."

"I am sorry. I promise you there will be no next time."

"You better promise your friends and everyone on-board. Everyone has been worrying about you."

"I am truly sorry."

I kept on apologizing, not knowing what else to say.

"Who saved us?" I asked curiously.

"An android we usually keep for rescue mission. But, it is not important for you to know right now," Eva said. "Right now, we have a situation."

"What is the situation?"

"The mission to Zeptune is aborted."

20

"I beg your pardon?" I frowned.

"Yesterday, we received a transmission that the Chinese unintentionally struck one of their own satellites. The side effect is a chain reaction of debris flying through space. The chain reaction is out of control. Many of our satellites are down. We had a communication blackout with the company. The high-speed debris will be in our route any moment. We are forced to change our route," Eva explained.

I was disappointed.

"So, are we heading back to Earth?" I asked.

"Unlikely, the debris storm is on the way. The satellites in that attitude were down," Eva replied.

"What are we going to do now?"

"We are going to land in one of the closest planets to conserve fuel for our return trip."

"Which planet are we going to land?"

"ED-209."

Just as Eva was about to turn around, a picture fell out of her purse and landed on one of the white tiles on the ground.

I reached out from my bed to pick up the photo.

It was a vintage photo with Eva and a little girl celebrating a birthday.

The little girl has long blond hair and big green eyes. She had the most innocent and genuine smile I have ever seen.

"Very cute. What is her name?" I said, carefully handed the photo back to Eva.

"Her name is Venus." Eva smiled.

All of a sudden, the solemn look on Eva faded.

"Nice name. It is the name of a Roman goddess of beauty and love. No wonder she looks so adorable and full of life," I appraised.

"She was four when I left her for a space mission." Eva forced a smile. "I remembered I used to cradle her in my arms, swaddled her in a blanket, singing songs to put her into sleep. She is such a beautiful baby girl."

"Where is she now?" I pursued.

"She died at the age of seventy six." Eva looked sad, tears welled her eyes.

"Huh? Seventy six?" I cried in disbelief.

"Ironic, isn't it." Eva wiped her tears off her face. "She was married. Divorced. No children. Her final wish was to see me one day. But, it never happened… I took too long. It was too late."

"I am sorry about your daughter," I apologized in a whisper.

"How about you? What is your story? What brought you to space?" Eva asked.

"I am an orphan. My parents left me for space when I

was four. They never returned. One of the reasons I am in space is to find them. I know it sounds silly. I know there is only a slim chance. But, I really want to see them again. I really want to know why they broke their promise," I revealed.

Eva studied at me for a long moment with her round blue eyes.

"Nobody can love you more than your parents. No love is greater than mom's love. No care is greater than dad's care," Eva said.

"Really?"

"I can assure you that. I am a mother myself. Oh well, I think I guess we do have something in common after all." Eva gave me a genuine smile.

***

It has been sixty hours since we returned to Sudoku.

To me, the concept of "day" has become a little bit abstract.

Since everyone has been conditioned to a 24-hour daily cycle on Earth, the rhythm of waking and sleeping in a fixed schedule is hard-wired in our brains.

Peter was sleeping soundly in his sleeping bag. A bubble contacted and expanded around his nose.

Tommy and Sol had their limbs floating at odd angles.

Molly and Karen were in a fetus-like posture in their sleeping bag.

A "morning" alarm stirred us out of the bed to begin our day.

Everyone got ready and gathered in the space canteen through different corridors.

The canteen was artistic, clean and spacious. There were twelve round, white tables aligned evenly in the room. In the center of the room was one giant vending machine, mounted from floor to ceiling like a pillar. The control panel had numerous options that had the intelligence to recommend the breakfast we like based on our past selections.

I ordered my favorite Double Quarter Pounder hamburger.

When I turned around, I saw Eva and a few marines sitting in one of the tables, having their breakfast.

I went over to greet her. And she said she would see us all for morning briefing after breakfast.

"So, what happens next?" Karen and Molly raised their ears like bugs bunny as Tommy was busy making up stories on how he saved everyone from the giant wave on Wiur.

"The wave was like a mountain. I ignored the danger and swam towards Nova and the Japanese dude. Then I dragged them all the way back to the mouth of the dropship and swung them back inside like Hercules, and then slid the door shut. I swear to God if I hesitated for even a second, you wouldn't be seeing us returning in one piece," Tommy exaggerated.

"Hey, I thought I was the one who shut that door," Sol complained.

"You were only checking if I shut it properly." Tommy threw his buddy a wink.

"I am glad that I made the right decision by staying in Suduko." Karen shivered.

"Yes. You are right." Molly agreed. "By the way, where is Peter?"

Peter sat at the opposite side of the round table by himself. He knew Tommy too well. It is best to stay away from the bully.

"Tommy, who is that Dr. Cool you guys rescued?" Molly asked. "Has anyone even seen him?"

Everyone shook their head.

"I don't know. Maybe he is still sleeping." Tommy shrugged his shoulder.

Then we heard footsteps.

When we turned around, our eyes opened wide as an unfamiliar old man stood in the mouth of a corridor to the canteen. That man had grey-white hair. Wrinkles spread across his face as he greeted everyone in the room. He looked exhausted and weak, as if he has not been eating a proper meal for many days.

The worst of all, he had a strange smell that drew everyone away.

All of us paused our breakfast.

"Dr. Cool, this is captain Eva, welcome on board," Eva greeted the odd doctor, attempting to break the ice.

But, the doctor ignored her, shook his head, and walked away.

"Excuse me." Eva frowned.

The atmosphere turned awkward.

Everyone stared at the strange doctor for his odd behavior.

He was not appreciative we risked our life saving him.

"That is rude," Karen muttered, chewing her salad.

"That is not rude. That is strange," Molly corrected.

"Dr. Strange," Tommy joked.

"Na. He looked like someone escaped from a mental

hospital. He can never be Dr. Strange," Sol said.

Everyone in our table giggled at his lame joke.

"Hey Peter, come and join our table." I gestured gently.

But Peter shook his head and refused.

Usually, Peter is quite obedient. He always does as I say. Maybe when Tommy is around, this is a different story. They never get along with each other.

My eyes focused on the odd doctor.

He looked frustrated. He was murmuring to himself.

No one understands what he is trying to say.

My intuition tells me there must be some stories behind that.

I wonder what he went through.

***

"This is commercial vessel Suduko, registration number MSV-9120, calling ED-209 traffic control. Over. We request immediate permission to transfer passengers port-side," Eva called over the radio.

Static filled the air.

No response.

"Hello. This is Captain Eva from commercial vessel Suduko. I repeat. We request immediate permission to transfer passengers port-side."

Still no response.

"It has been eighty hours. Why isn't ED-209 responding?" Eva puzzled.

"It seems that ED-209 communication system is pretty screw up too," a marine next to her complained. The nametag on his shoulder was the name Ian.

"Eva, what is the visual below?" Ian asked.

"ED-209 is kind of mountainous and there has been volcanic activity. Other than that, most of the other readings are unreadable." Eva threw a few buttons to reveal the geography on the screen.

"I thought that the chain reaction of debris wouldn't affect our communication with ED-209. It is not even in that route," Ian speculated.

"I thought so, too. But, there are many reasons our communication with them is blocked, like big storms or failed relay for example," Eva guessed.

Eva leaned back on her captain chair. She had her hands crossed behind her head. Thinking.

"Eighty hours is probably a record we have been out of contact with any of our colonies," Ian assured.

Ian is right.

But, what is going on?

Eva has a bad feeling about this.

She went over the files of ED-209.

Apparently, ED-209 is the first planet Zirgin Galactic successfully terraformed into a suitable environment for large-scale human habitation. It housed over two hundred people. There were fifty atmospheric processing planets constructed and installed around the perimeter of the Gateway Station to make the air breathable.

Two hundred people...

The conversation she had in the meeting room of interstellar cruiser ST-132 came back to her mind.

There have been colonists living there for almost a decade. The military received no complains from them about it...

Yeah right. The company doesn't believe a word she

says.

They mocked her.

They humiliated her.

They think she is telling them some kind of joke.

They even banned her ICC license as commercial flight officer, and now, they are pleading with her to come back to ED-209 to check it out.

The company is as unpredictable as the weather forecast.

Well, Eva can't blame them. She is suffering from severe memory lapse after long-term hypersleep.

All she could remember was that she and her crew on a M-class star freighter carried precious minerals back to the base. On the way home, they were redirected by the company to carry out an investigation on a SOS signal on ED-209. Something happened to the investigation team. But, they came back in one piece. Then, something happened… something terrible happened that forced her to blow the entire ship.

She tried to puzzle the scattered memories back together.

But, they were like fragments of broken glass.

She wants to forget them.

But every night, she is awakened by bad dreams. Terrifying dreams.

That is why she eventually listened to Kurt to get back on the horse to face the truth.

She wanted to find out why she blew up the M-class star freighter.

She wants to prove that she is innocent and did not kill her own crew.

"Eva, are you okay?" Ian asked.

"Eva, the history files of the company suggested to land in these coordinates in case of communication failure with ED-209 facility due to bad weather," Okaa-san suggested.

Eva checked the coordinates on the screen.

Somehow, they looked familiar.

The dots joined together to form a perfect triangle… much like Bermuda Triangle in the Atlantic Ocean.

"A devil triangle in ED-209 and an eighty hours lost of communication. This just keeps getting better and better," Eva whispered to herself.

Eva thought about her unsuspecting crew.

She wondered why the company is only sending orphans to accompany them in this mission.

What is the company planning?

Eva sat firmly in the pilot seat.

Bright light shone on her from the windows above her head. It was a collapsing star in a black hole so not even light could escape.

When she lowered her head to the cockpit, Sudoku was already entering the atmosphere of ED-209.

PART 3

21

The hum of Suduko's dropship turned into a metallic shriek as it hit the atmosphere of ED-209. It slewed wickedly from side to side before finally becoming steady.

Everyone, except Tommy, buckled up, held onto the safety rig, and locked on their seat. As usual, he was busy teasing, showing off the weapons as a newly joined marine.

I looked at Eva.

She was concentrating on piloting.

"We are in the pipe, five by five," Eva confirmed as our dropship thrusted forward.

Tommy howled like a werewolf as we plunged down straight abruptly before stabilizing.

I gritted my teeth as the atmosphere debris scraped the hull.

"Rough air ahead," Eva warned.

The dropship shook violently and Tommy staggered.

"Get back in here, Son. I rather you do not die on the first day of my command," Ian scolded.

"Don't worry, Captain. I am ready. I hope we have more action than to terraform," Tommy replied and walked towards Peter. "Hey Peter! Don't you worry, my buddy marines and I will protect you. Check this out, M41-B pulse rifle, with ultra-light titanium aluminum casting. It can fry anything with its 10 millimeter by 24 explosive rounds even at a long distance."

Peter turned away from him, thinking he is an idiot.

Dr. Cool shook his head in a corner. He didn't talk to anyone the whole time.

I heard the gossip from the marines saying Eva had an argument with the Doctor before they decided to go to ED-209.

I wonder what happened.

A moment later, the retro-rockets kicked in, and the dropship further descended.

"Wowww!" Tommy lost his balance and felt flat on the ground.

"Here you go, handsome." Eva threw Tommy a wink.

"Get back here. Stop fooling around." Ian helped Tommy to get back on his feet and instructed him to sit.

The metallic shriek continued.

I stared outside the cockpit but could see nothing but mist and fog.

Water drops were running down randomly on the screen in a zig-zag pattern.

The visibility was way too low to see anything.

I wonder how did the residents in ED-209 terraform this place?

It seems that terraforming is very different from what the company propaganda is trying to portray.

I thought terraforming would be interesting.

Well, obviously, this is not the case.

I began to regret.

A hydraulic hiss from dropship interrupted my thoughts.

Eva studied the coordinates on the screen, and then she raised her head to search for something.

"Where is the marker beacon?" Eva wondered.

Unfortunately, the bad weather made everything way too hard to see.

A moment later, they saw scattered light from a distance.

Several colonial buildings began to appear in sight.

"Oh I see it now. Okaa-san, give me a slow circle of the complex," Eva commanded.

I looked outside the cockpit once more.

I thought I was staring at a world with black and grey.

When lightning struck, it revealed the silhouette of buildings in box structures.

From a distance, I saw a glass hemisphere, towering above everything else.

From below, I saw a few trailers parked outside a building.

The place looked abandoned.

It had power, but there were no visible activities below.

Maybe everyone is staying indoors to avoid the bad weather.

"The complexes still have power. Why aren't the citizens in ED-209 responding to my transmission?" Eva wondered.

"There is only one way to find out," Ian said as he motioned Eva to a flashing beacon below them.

Eva guided the dropship forward until it landed gently on the rocky ground.

A moment later, the cabin brightened into a comfortable bright-white glow.

Eva disengaged the door locks and stood up from her pilot seat.

Everyone unbuckled their seatbelt and stretched.

"Thanks for the roller coaster ride," Tommy said.

"Should I take this as a compliment?" Eva raised an eyebrow.

She led us to the starboard door and punched a code in the control pad.

Seconds later, the door hissed open.

A short ramp slid out with a rattle and clunked onto the rocky surface of the planet.

One by one, we followed Eva to descend the ramp.

There were twenty-five of us.

I just realized I don't even know most of their names.

The howling wind blew fiercely.

Rain paddled in our face.

Torrent of dust and grits blinded us.

Even in masks and hoods, we can hardly see anything.

Already, I could see the regretful look on Peter's face.

Perhaps terraforming other planets wasn't such a good idea after all.

"Marines, move in. The rest of us head back inside the control center of the dropship until the marines cleared the place," Eva shouted over the storm.

"Affirmative," the marines said.

It was raining heavily.

The ground was thick with mud.

There were a few abandoned vehicles in the midst outside of the complex.

The colonial marines spread out around the vehicles.

They quickened their pace to the nearest complex.

A solitary, familiar company logo of Zirgin Galactic glowed.

It was the South-East gate.

"First squad up," Captain Ian commanded. "Gordon, in the corridor, watch the rear."

The marines proceeded swiftly.

When the marines arrived at the entrance, it was seal shut.

"Second squad, move up," Captain Ian commanded. "Alex, run a bypass."

Alex moved swiftly to a control pad on the right. Then he opened up the lid and clipped the terminals of the unit with the alligator clips, connecting to his hacking device.

"Door lock disengaged," Alex reported.

The heavy metal barrier of the complex opened like the mouth of an almighty worm.

Dim. Hideous. Mysterious.

Then the marines went inside the shadow.

I focused on the abyss.

I don't have a good feeling about it.

I wonder how long are we going to stay…

22

We marines grouped in close formation.

They checked each corner cautiously.

Their shoulder torches illuminated their path.

Tommy and Sol were with them.

There were fourteen of them, split in two groups.

We were watching them through our monitors.

"Jesus, check this out." Tommy motioned us to his discovery.

The ceiling was down. Tattered wires were hanging. Water dribbled from a ruptured pipe. The metal grill flooring of the corridor had been ripped apart.

I swallowed hard.

Who could have done something like this?

"That is what happens if a company does not pay their workers enough to maintain this place," Sol joked.

"Second squad, move inside," Captain Ian signaled. "Tommy, Sol, take the upper level."

The second squad advanced into the complex.

Eva checked the marines' head-cam, observing the operation.

I looked at the others in the room.

Everyone focused on the monitors. Sweat trickled down our forehead. No one spoke a single word.

Tommy cautiously proceeded to the Level One, with Sol following from behind.

The place was eerily silent.

They could hear nothing but their own heavy footsteps thundering on the metal grill floor.

Apparently, the lights in Level One were damaged.

It was too dark to see.

"Tommy, Sol, you copying? Use your motion trackers," Captain Ian suggested.

"Affirmative."

Tommy and Sol advanced slowly.

The motion tracker remained static.

"This place is dead and damaged. Nothing unusual." Tommy yawned.

Nothing unusual? There should be colonists in here. This is unusual.

Just as Sol was about to continue his way, something on his head-cam showed in the corner of our eyes.

"Sol, wait! Get back. To your left," Eva requested.

Sol turned around as instructed.

Then he saw it too.

It was a large hole on the metal grill flooring.

"Guys, you are going to love this one." Tommy revealed another one with his head-cam.

This hole is much bigger.

It is big enough for an adult to fall through.

The frightening thing is that the hole melted through several levels…melted by strong acid.

I couldn't take my eyes off the burn site.
A wave of unknown fear sent chills down my spine.
All of a sudden, everything looked unreal.
What could have done something like this?
Where is everyone?

23

Captain Ian carefully stepped around the acid-eaten floor, regrouped after a series of searches.

"The area is secured. Eva, you and the rest of the team can come in," Ian confirmed.

I dropped my mouth open.

"Eva, are we sure - " I tried to speak, but Eva dismissed me.

"Didn't you hear what the captain says?" Eva said.

Strange.

Molly and Karen swallowed hard.

Peter looked at me with those worried eyes.

"I thought we are here to terraform new planets," Peter whispered. "Are we going to be all right?"

Since Dr. Cool warned us about ED-209, I looked at him for clues, but he snickered and turned away.

"Silly boy, Of course we will be okay. We are just going to stay here for a while." I pretended.

The truth is, by the look of it, I do not know how long we are going to stay.

The rain got heavier.

Purplish blue lightning cut the sky zig-zag.

Eva and the rest of us met up with the marines at the entrance of the South-East gate.

Captain Ian organized two marines to fix the power and get the CPU online.

"How are we doing?" Eva asked.

"The South-East gate is cleared. The research lab is still unchecked. But, we can use the operation room as our temporary base," Captain Ian reported.

"Still no signs of any colonists?" Eva puzzled.

The marines shook their head.

"Strange. We have searched almost everywhere. This placed looked deserted. There should be around two hundred people. And it is in the middle of a storm. Where else can they stay?" Tommy asked.

"Actually, there is one place we haven't checked yet," Sol reported.

"What is it?" Captain Ian asked.

"It is the lab," Sol said.

"Why didn't we check the lab in the first place?" Eva wondered.

"Because the door requires a special biometric pass-code," Sol looked at Dr. Cool and said.

"Yeah. You are right. Dr. Cool is a key researcher in ED-209. He should be able to get us in," Hiroyuki agreed.

Dr. Cool swallowed hard.

He studied us for a long while.

It was as if he had something secretive he wants to

keep from us.

"I am afraid I cannot do that."

24

"Why not?" Eva frowned.

Just when Eva pursued to challenge the doctor, a marine raced towards us breathlessly.

"Captain, you have to see this. We have located the colonists," the marine interrupted.

We hurried behind the marine to the operation room.

When we arrived, we saw a dozen marines already lining up in place.

"Captain, Look. Over here. Their personal data transmitters suggest that are all inside this atmospheric processing plant fifteen miles north of this complex," one of the marines motioned us to a computer screen.

"Odd. Why are the colonists gathering in the atmospheric processing plant?" Molly doubted.

"Maybe there is a malfunction somewhere," Karen speculated.

"Even if there is a malfunction, it does not take everyone to go and fix it. Not in this weather. It is turbulent outside," Peter disputed.

"Then I am not sure." Karen shrugged.

"That explains why they have lost contact with us. Eva, we will head to the atmospheric generator. You and the others will stay here until we return," Ian suggested.

"Be careful." Eva looked at Ian and warned.

"Marines, we are moving out."

***

Hours went by after the marines left for the rescue mission.

Even though the complex had power restored, the damage and the ghostly dribbling water sound in the background still gave me the creeps.

Maybe I just felt less secure without the marines.

"They have been gone for a long time," Peter whispered.

"Don't worry. They will be all right." I comforted him, lowering my head.

The wind howled brutally outside the complex.

I began to worry about Tommy and Sol.

They were with the marines outside.

A dreadful fear had been building in us.

"I am scared. I want to go back to Earth." Peter's eyes meet my gaze.

"You are a big boy now. You must learn to be strong. Besides, we are just going to stay here for a short while, remember?" I said.

I looked at Eva.

She had her back facing me while talking to Dr. Cool.

"Doctor, now tell me. What happened in this place?" Eva demanded.

"I don't remember a thing," Dr. Cool declined.

"Don't remember? Or you just don't want to tell us. We received a SOS from you when you crashed landed into the water world of Wiur. We risked our life saving you," Eva said.

"I did not request your help. Besides, I did warn you in that transmission to stay away from ED209," Dr. Cool spoke.

"This is absurd. The company policy requires any potential distress signal must be investigated. I feel I have made the wrong choice saving you. Tell me what is going on!" Eva shouted.

"Captain Eva. Some secrets are meant to stay secret forever. You and your troops shouldn't be here. It is a big mistake."

25

Captain Ian steered the wheel of a heavy crawler and headed to the atmospheric processing unit.

The heavy crawler rumbled and rattled as it crawled on the uneven terrain of ED-209.

In this vast interior of the crawler was his squad of marines, lined up on the benches.

"Tell me something. Has anyone asked why we are being sent along on this excursion?" Ian asked, trying to break the ice.

"I did ask. We were supposed to go to Zuptune. All of a sudden, we received a distress call from Wiur. Then a space storm forced us to change our route and land on ED-209," Tommy said.

"The funny thing is that Dr. Kim, who is supposed to be our supervisor, was swapped with Eva," Sol complained.

"Funny." Ian arched an eyebrow.

"Funny?" Tommy was confused.

"Never heard of Zuptune before," Ian said, turning around and asking the other marines. "Boys, have anyone of you heard of Zuptune?"

"I know Neptune, but Zuptune doesn't ring bell," Alex said.

"Huh? That is strange. Then what operation were you on?" Sol asked.

"We were under direct order from General Muesel to protect Eva on her investigation in ED-209," Ian said. "Otherwise, what else do you think we would be doing in this rock?"

Sol and Tommy exchanged glances with each other.

Something isn't right.

"It is Zirgin Galactic, if that explain it all," a marine at the back yelled.

The atmospheric storm continued.

The gale raged.

The crawler dipped into a swallow muddy pit and then climbed back out of it again.

The blowing grit hit the metal of the crawler and sang a high pitch melody.

For a few seconds, the marines saw nothing beyond the windshield.

"Bloody marvelous." Ian gritted his teeth.

The storm was too strong.

He wondered how the two hundred colonists managed to move to the atmospheric processing unit.

It is mission impossible in this kind of weather.

He called Eva to inform her they are being held up by the storm.

But, all he could hear was static in response.

"Great." Ian sighed. "Is this always like this in ED-209?"

"Captain, look." Alex pointed at a glass hemisphere behind a wind-driven swirl of grit.

Flash of lightning revealed the building.

Thunder rolled overhead like the fury of gods.

The marines stared through the windshield.

Ominous. Haunted.

They could feel chills in their bones.

Back on Earth, Tommy loved to explore the woods with Sol at night. They loved to do that because rumors say that there were treasures in the woods not far from St George Orphan School. So, they ignored Miss O' Connor's warning even though she forbid them to go. One night, they sneaked out as usual. They had an ominous feeling, but they ignored it. During their exploration, the woods turned misty. They couldn't find their way out. They were lost in the woods for three days.

Right now, it is the same gut feeling screaming at them to go away.

"Looks like we have found what we are after," Ian spoke.

He hit the accelerator and the crawler roared through the muddy ground.

A moment later, they arrived at the entrance.

"Move it!" Ian bellowed and urged the marines to get ready.

He parked and exited the crawler first. Alex next. And the rest of the marines followed.

"Whoa." Tommy staggered as the gale blew him.

"Are you all right?" Alex helped him to regain his balance, but Tommy could barely hear what he said. His voice was carried away by the wind.

They stormed inside the atmospheric processing unit. Minutes later, everyone was indoors.

"I hope our crawler won't get blown away," Sol joked.

Captain Ian head counted the marines.

He arranged two marines, Dante and Virgil, to stay back on the crawlers and the rest of the squad to follow him.

"This place is the size of a stadium," Paris, one of the marines, exclaimed.

"The atmospheric processing unit is big for a reason. It is designed to convert inhospitable atmosphere into one that is suitable for the entire colony. There are sixty of these units on ED-209," Ian said.

"Captain, how does it work?" another marine called Russell asked.

"They do something to the air, clean it, treat it, to make it breathable. I don't really know. We are marines, not scientists," Ian replied vaguely.

He led his squad deeper and deeper beneath the building.

The place darkened.

Blackness slowly came, stealing their ability to see.

Even with the map, it is a labyrinth in here.

The marines switched on their helmet lamp to illuminate the place.

"Man, it is hot in here. Hot and humid," Paris complained. Sweat trickled down his back.

The marines swept their spot of light at the ceiling.

The complicated piping and ductwork in the wall and ceiling formed strange typography.

Tommy focused on his motion tracker. Green light

cast a glow on his face.

BEEP.

"Signals."

"Position, Tommy."

"Sub-levels three."

The marines increased their pace.

They took a few turns and then decided to follow a branch corridor that was usually used by the maintenance workers.

Halfway through the corridor, they saw a service elevator.

The dim light on the ceiling revealed there was gas leakage on the ducts.

"The elevator can take six of us at most. We will have to split," Alex advised.

"Good thinking," Ian agreed. "We will locate where the colonists are. Then we will evacuate. Hope this freight elevator is robust enough."

"Should we take the stairs?" Alex asked.

"No. Tommy, Sol, Paris, Nguyen, Roger and Chris, come with me. The rest will stay. No one goes exploring. Just secure the area around the elevator and wait for us," Ian commanded.

"Copy that."

"All right, get moving."

***

The elevator rumbled and clattered as the rusty door slid closed.

It clanged and began to descend.

Tommy slumped against the inside of the elevator.

The rest of the marines tilted their head and focused on the floor display.

The industrial noises in the atmospheric processing unit made it almost indistinguishable to the rattling sound of the elevator.

BEEP, BEEP.

The pinging sound of the motion tracker intensified.

"This must be where the colonists are."

A moment later, they arrived at the basement.

Ian was the first one to step out of the elevator, with Chris a quick second.

One by one, the marines followed.

"This way," Ian said as he led his squad to a dark corridor ahead of them.

On the right, a few generators were installed behind the rusted wire meshes.

On the left, they saw shafts of blue light filter through the vents.

Ian turned one corner after another.

"This place is like a labyrinth," Nguyen complained. "It is worse than getting lost in the woods in Vietnam."

"It is getting hotter and hotter too," Chris whined.

"No wonder the colonists stay here in the sub level - to escape the cold weather up there," Paris added.

BEEP, BEEP, BEEP.

"The colonists must be up ahead," Ian announced.

The marines increased their pace towards the sound.

"Wait up!" Tommy shouted, being left behind.

The floor was a bit slippery, so he rested his hand on the wall to steady himself.

"What the?"

Tommy touched something wet and sticky.

So, he shifted his shoulder lamp to illuminate the wall.

To his surprise, his palm was covered with strands of a thick, slimy substance.

It felt like some kind of gelatinous resin or glue.

Green. Grey. Opaque.

Gross.

Who would have left done something like this on the wall?

"Captain Ian, look what I found," Tommy shouted.

No reply.

They were too far ahead.

Tommy ignored the peculiar substances and hurried after his team.

The spot light of his shoulder lamp darted left and right in blackness.

The shuffle of his footsteps echoed in the dark corridor.

"Sol, you gotta to see - ."

Just as Tommy was about to regroup with the rest of the marines ahead, he saw everyone stood still. Head tilted. Their eyes bulged. Their mouths dropped in disbelief.

Circles of spotlights were dancing randomly on the ceiling.

"This…..this is unreal," Sol stammered in a whisper.

The walls. The corridor. The floor. Everything was covered with some type of dark, resinous substances.

Strange, complex ridges and curves crisscrossing made the whole place look like some kind of giant insect hive.

The shadow. The patterns. The whole chamber made them feel like it was full of menace.

Roger dropped to his knee and felt the ground with his fingers.

"It feels like some kind of solidified resin. And it … it seems to be pulsing. It…it seems like the ground is alive." Roger almost choked out.

"Very funny." Sol coughed.

"Captain, what do you think happened here?" Paris spoke quietly.

Captain Ian paused for a long moment. His eyes couldn't take off the slithering patterns on the ceiling.

"I don't know," Ian whispered, staying sharp.

"Should we take some resin sample back to the base?" Chris suggested.

"No one touches anything," Ian ordered anxiously.

The marines continued to move.

They shone their shoulder lamp around and studied the chamber.

The light revealed a thin layer of bluish mist covering the floor.

"It is weirdly humid in here," Paris said.

"Maybe the atmospheric processing unit is drawing moisture from the outside, and retaining it in the chamber," Ian guessed.

BEEP, BEEP, BEEP.

The motion tracker beeped continuously.

A tiny red dot below the main screen display began to illuminate.

Then they heard a tiny voice.

A sad voice filled with sorrow, whining in darkness. "Kill me … kill me please," the voice begged.

26

"A survivor!"

Roger shouted and gestured the rest of the marines to come over to the wall.

"Oh my god." Tommy covered his mouth in fright.

Adrenaline rose inside him.

He was staring at an abomination - a survivor in a cocoon, pleading for death.

Half human. Half egg.

His entire body formed a hard, crisscrossing shell, attached to the wall.

Ooze was dripping from his hair and face.

The only thing that still appeared human was his head.

"Kill me…" the colonist moaned.

"Wh-what happened to you? Where are the others?" Ian asked, stunned by his discovery.

The colonist slowly tilted his head to the left.

Next to him were barely recognizable cocooned colonists, who seemed to be undergoing some sort of metamorphosis…

"Don't worry, hang it there. We will get you out of here," Ian assured.

Tommy looked at the cocoons in disgust.

How are we going to get them out of here?

Their egg-shaped cocooned bodies latched on the wall, on the ceiling.

It is hard to believe they were once humans who lived and breathed.

No wonder the company had lost contact with the colonists.

What happened in ED209?

27

"D r. Cool, tell me please. We have the right to know. Why did you warn us to stay away from ED-209?" I asked curiously.

Dr. Cool gazed at Eva for a moment and then turned to us.

"Kid, I thank you for saving my life. But, you don't belong in here. This is no place for kids," Dr. Cool replied.

"What do you mean this is no place for kids? We are kids on a mission to terraform Zuptune. We are forced to land here temporarily because of the debris storm in our route to Zuptune," I argued.

"Really? Is that what you were told?" Dr. Cool challenged.

"Yes. So? We are doing this for a cause," I said.

"You cannot afford to be so naive to believe everything the company told you," Dr. Cool mocked.

"What you are trying to say?" Molly wondered.

"All of you are here because of this woman." Dr. Cool pointed at Eva.

Eva looked guilty.

"It is she who brought all of you here," Dr. Cool clarified. "Captain Eva, you have forgotten everything in your past, haven't you?" Dr. Cool tested.

"I….umm." Eva tried to remember, but her memories scattered like fragments of broken glass.

"There you go," Dr. Cool said.

"How much do you know about my past?" Eva challenged.

28

"You were a logistics officer in an M-class star freighter. You were on a mission to transport rare minerals back to Earth eighty years ago. During your voyage, for some unknown reason, you blew up the ship. The company lost a lot of money. It was a black mark in the company's record. I remembered reading about you and your ship when I was a kid. We used to call you crazy woman in space," Dr. Cool mocked.

Eva felt guilty.

I studied Eva silently.

Why would she do that?

"Why did you do it? Why did you kill everyone onboard in that freighter?" Dr. Cool challenged.

"I… I didn't kill them," Eva's voice trembled.

She was angry, but sorrowful and regretful.

The strong motherhood figure of Eva crumbled.

Her hands trembled. She was becoming emotionally unstable.

"Do you know the crew members' family are waiting for them to come home?" Dr. Cool pushed further.

"I am telling you now I didn't kill them! It killed them." Eva broke down, shouting in rage.

"So, what is it?" Dr. Cool demanded.

"I don't know. I don't remember. Go away." Eva kneeled down, covering her ears in both hands.

Our strong image of Eva was suddenly replaced by a woman troubled by her remorseful past. All of a sudden, she became like a completely foreign person to the one we know.

"Leave her alone!" I scolded.

I went over to Eva and wrapped my hands around her to soothe her.

Others came over to join me.

"I don't know what happened in your past. But, it is going to be all right."

We comforted Eva.

"No… it is not all right. I came here to face my past. I came here to find out why I blew up the ship." Eva sobbed.

"What are you saying?" Peter was confused.

"I am saying I feel sorry for all of you to be on board," Eva said.

Suddenly, a wet and squishy sound from the end of the corridor drew our attention.

"What is that?" Molly's voice came out frightened.

The marines were gone. No colonists were found. Who could it possibly be?

Everyone exited the room into the corridor.

Step by step, we followed and traced the origin of the sound.

Our hearts were pounding.

Everyone, except Dr. Cool, appeared nervous.

"It…it seems to be coming from the lab," Karen stammered.

"The only part of the complex the marines have not searched," Hiroyuki confirmed.

"Do you think it can be a colonist?" I speculated.

"No. Otherwise, the marines' motion sensors could have pick that up," Eva rejected softly.

"Dr. Cool, can you finally open that door for us?" Hiroyuki demanded.

"Are you sure you want me to open that door?" Dr. Cool said reluctantly.

"Yes. Why not? Hurry up. There could be someone in there," Molly and Karen demanded.

Peter stayed behind me.

He shook my sleeves and pulled me back.

"I don't think it is a good idea," he spoke.

"Very well. As you wish," Dr. Cool said coldly.

29

Step by step, we approached the metallic door of the research lab.

The constant dribbling sound of water was abnormally loud. The tattered wires overhung in the ceiling reminded me of snakes.

Even we were in a group, I felt my heartbeat quicken.

I looked at Dr. Cool the whole time.

I wondered what secrets he is keeping from us.

I wonder what made him flee.

Why did the colonists leave this place for the atmospheric processing unit?

One way or the other, he must know something about what happened to this place.

Perhaps the answer lies inside this research lab.

Dr. Cool rested his chin on a stand for a special biometric scan.

Slowly, the metallic door swung open.

The room was white and vast.

We did not find anyone. No colonists.

In the middle of the room was a large square bench.

A brown-black, leathery egg–like a capsule with black spots was placed at the center of the table. Pulsing. The egg was roughly two and a half feet tall. At the base of the egg were plant-like roots that twisted and tangled on the surface of the bench.

Everyone dropped their mouth open in disbelief.

We all looked at Dr. Cool, demanding an explanation.

"Don't look at me like this. I am not the one who laid it. It was the colonists who brought this back," Dr. Cool said.

"The colonists?" I queried.

"They were under direct order from Zirgin Galactic to check out specific coordinates from ED-209 – the same coordinates that Eva's ship had been to eighty years ago," Dr. Cool explained.

"Eva, do you know about these?"

Eva shook her head.

"I didn't land on ED-209 in person. My crew members did," Eva spoke softly.

She focused on the pulsing egg.

She was absorbed in her own thoughts.

Scattered memories came back to her mind like a river of pain.

"I shouldn't have told the company what happened," Eva murmured regretfully. "I remember it now. It…it is this thing that annihilated my whole crew."

Slowly, Eva became emotionally unstable.

"It is this thing…it is this thing," Eva said repeatedly.

We looked worried.

"Eva, are you okay?" we asked.

"An egg annihilated your whole crew? I really want to

know how it did that," Hiroyuki cried in disbelief.

Hiroyuki ran bravely towards the egg.

"Hiroyuki, no. We don't know what it is yet."

Dr. Cool shook his head, crossed his arms, smiling.

"Foolish boy."

Molly, Karen and I tried to pull Hiroyuki back, but we lost our balance and missed.

He is too impulsive.

When I looked at Hiroyuki again, he was already near the egg.

"See, there is nothing to be afraid of." Hiroyuki turned back and teased.

"Get back!" Eva snapped.

Suddenly, a hissing sound from within the egg drew Hiroyuki's attention.

Hiroyuki turned back. He lowered his head and saw the four petal-like lips at the top of the ovoid, leathery egg opening. Strings of mucous were hanging from the petals as it split apart.

Hiroyuki was paralyzed.

His eyes wide opened in fright.

"Oh my god. Look out!"

A dark object lunged at him from the egg and latched onto his face.

The next thing he heard was his own scream.

30

"Hiroyuki, noooooooooo!"

Eva tried to save Hiroyuki, but she was too late.

Everyone backed off when we saw the creature that latched onto Hiroyuki's face.

The creature is like an arachnid, beige in color. It is around three meters long. Its body resembles a pair of skeletal hands with eight webbed finger-like digits, fused with a spine-like tail.

Within seconds, Hiroyuki collapsed onto the ground. Unconscious.

"Oh my god!" Molly backed off to the closest wall and covered her mouth.

Karen's eyes opened wide in disbelief, frozen in terror.

I looked at Peter and Eva. They were paralyzed like me.

"I warned all of you not to go inside the lab," Dr. Cool said coldly.

"You...you warned us? You never told us what is inside," Eva said.

"Will you ever listen? Some secrets are meant to stay

secret forever from the public," Dr. Cool uttered a horrible laugh. He is insane.

I took one small step towards Hiroyuki, then another.

I looked at poor Hiroyuki as the creature wrapped its digits around his neck and head.

Tighter and tighter.

It was trying to suffocate him…

"People, do something!" I said.

I took a deep breath and attempted to remove the creature from Hiroyuki.

But, Dr. Cool stopped me from behind.

"Stop!" Dr. Cool bellowed.

Stop? Are you trying to ask me to watch my friend slowly strangled to death by it? This creature is trying to kill him.

"Why?" I yelled back.

"Do you know you will kill him by removing the creature?" Dr. Cool said.

"What did you just say?"

"I said. If you remove it by force, the creature will kill him instantly," Dr. Cool explained.

"How do you know?" Eva challenged.

"Because it was what happened to the colonists in ED-209," Dr. Cool replied.

Everyone looked at Dr. Cool in shock.

"Maybe I should start from the beginning." Dr. Cool tilted his glasses and began to speak.

PART 4

31

"Alan, stop hiding!" Madeline whined. She had been crawling in the ceiling air vent for almost an hour, playing hide and seek with other children.

Staying stealth from the adults and watching them from above the ceiling was the fun part of their adventure.

Sometimes, they could even eavesdrop on secrets they aren't supposed to hear.

This is the good side of being in ED-209.

The ceiling vent is like a labyrinth.

It is the best place for hide and seek.

Right after Madeline's nine-year-old birthday, Madeline's parents had finally been granted a permit to live and work in space by the government. Zirgin Galactic offered them a high paying job there. So, they left the overpopulated Earth behind and migrated to this distant planet called ED-209.

It was a scary thought at first.

But, they settled eventually anyway.

Since then, Madeline and her eleven-year-old brother,

Alan, lived in ED-209, they got even less chance to see their parents. Their parents are always away. Whenever they asked them what they were doing, the standard reply was that they were busy.

So, that is why she and her brother invented this hide and seek game in the ceiling air vent. In the game, someone plays as the monster, who will then find other kids and turn them into a monster until everyone is found.

Once, they managed to scare even the adults by making strange growling noises in the vent. They could never forget how the frightened adults raced off from the compartment to call for the colonial marines for help. Scaring adults was the best.

There were no such things as monsters in this world. No real ones.

That is what the adults have been telling them. But, the truth is that the adults believe in monster themselves. Funny.

"Madeline, you give up so easily," Alan's voice boomed from behind her.

"This is not fair," Madeline complained.

"What is so unfair about it?" Alan asked.

"You cheated," Madeline accused.

"How can I cheat in hide and seek?" Alan denied.

"I don't know. Andrew says you cheated," Madeline continued.

"Yeah right. I just know the place better than anyone else," Alan said, leaning his back against the metal plate of the vent.

"Alan, you must be really bored," Andrew said. He is

Madeline and Alan's best friend in ED-209. They met on the first day on the planet.

"Aren't you bored? Mom and Dad took us all the way here from Earth. We used to go to school. In here, we aren't doing anything," Alan said.

"Na. We did pretty cool stuff. Remember we met that old doctor in the white lab coat. He showed us how to walk on liquid," Andrew sounded excited.

"Oh, you mean Dr. Cool? He is awesome," Alan sounded excited.

"Exactly."

"But the thing is that he spent all the time in his lab with his science experiments. To be honest with you, he gives me the creeps sometimes the way he grins," Alan said.

"Whatever. I am sleepy. By the way, is Mom and Dad back yet?" Madeline yawned.

Alan checked his watch.

"This is unusual. It is almost ten at night. I am thinking Mom and Dad have been gone for an awfully long time," Alan replied.

***

Shuffle of heavy footsteps echoed in the corridor of the South-East gate of the complex in ED-209.

A group of colonial marines were carrying someone on a stretcher and hurried towards the medical bay.

"Move. Out of the way," the marines bellowed at the suspicious crowds who gathered to see what is happening.

"Hurry. Call the doctor," one of the marines ordered

the nurse at the entrance.

Cindy, Madeline's mother, was racing beside the marines.

Worried. Terrified. Frustrated.

She couldn't take her eyes off her unconscious husband, lying on the stretcher, with an unknown creature attached to his face.

"Save my husband," Cindy pleaded, sobbing.

The crowd was nervous. Some of them twisted their face in disgust. Some immediately backed away when they saw this hideous creature with eight webbed fingers wrapped around Tim's face.

The marines turned a few corners and finally arrived at the entrance of the medical bay.

"Madam, you have to let the doctors do their job. I am afraid you have to stay outside," a nurse insisted.

"Tim needs me. Please. Let me in," Cindy pleaded.

The marines felt sympathy for Cindy.

"I understand that. But, if you really want to help your husband, the best way is to let the doctor takes care of him," one of the marines comforted her.

"Let her in," a doctor, appearing from the medical bay, said.

"Please. Dr. Cool. You need to help Tim. You need to take that thing off his face. You need to take that thing off his face," Cindy repeated.

"I will do everything I can," Dr. Cool said.

Dr. Cool ordered the marines to stay outside the medical bay and to stand by.

He and a few other doctors gathered around the stretcher to examine the creature that latched on Tim's face.

"I have never seen anything like this before," Dr. Cool whispered.

His assistant tried to use a medical clamp to remove the creature.

But, as soon as the clamp touched the creatures, it latched even tighter around Tim's neck.

"Stop. It will suffocate him," Dr. Cool ordered.

"Isn't it suffocating Tim already?" Cindy asked nervously.

"No. Tim is still alive. If the creature tries to suffocate him, he would be dead already," Dr. Cool said, cross one arm, thinking.

He ordered his assistance to take X-rays of Tim.

They looked at the display on the monitor.

Confused.

Dr. Cool pointed at the two, long tentacles.

One extended through the host's nasal cavity and the other through the esophagus.

"I know why Tim still survive," Dr. Cool said as pointed at the host's trachea.

"Why?" Cindy asked.

"It is doing the breathing for him."

32

"Mommy, what happened to Daddy?" Madeline worried.

"Daddy is going to be okay. He is just a little bit sick. So, he needs to see a doctor," Cindy explained, trying to stay calm.

"Where is Daddy? I want to see him. I want to see him," Alan whined.

"Alan, quiet," Cindy said, putting a finger to her lips to shush him. "Daddy is in the medical lab. He needs rest."

"But I heard Mr. Anderson next door says some bad thing happened to Daddy," Alan protested.

"Don't listen to rumor. Daddy is going to be fine. Don't be afraid." Cindy exhaled. Exhausted. She didn't expect her son to know.

"Be brave," Madeline looked straight at Alan and said.

"Kids. Get some sleep. It had been a long day." Cindy sighed.

She tucked her two kids into bed.

Tim. You have to be okay. You need to be okay. The children are waiting for you. She prayed.

A moment later, a sudden door knock interrupted her thoughts.

Cindy put on her slippers. She hurried to the front door of their compartment to see who was there.

Madeline rubbed her eyes with her knuckles.

Shaft of white light from the half opened door blinded her.

"Is it Mrs. Cindy Shaun?"

"Yes. It is me. How can I help you?"

"The General is waiting for you upstairs in the board room. He wants to know exactly what happened out there. He wants you to brief him about what have you seen. Every detail you remember is going to be important."

***

"Alan, wake up," Madeline whispered in Alan's ears.

Alan turned his back to his sister. He pulled the rest of the blanket towards him and wrapped it around his head. His face burrowed in his pillow like an emu buries its head in the sand.

"Hey, stop stealing my blanket," Madeline whined.

"Let me sleep," Alan snored.

A bubble contracted and expanded on his left nose.

It was too comfortable for him to get out of bed.

"Mommy is gone. I am scared." Madeline sat up in bed.

Alan ignored her.

A message ringtone from their best friend, Andrew, distracted her.

She grabbed the phone at the cupboard next to her

bed.

The message reads: Hey. Come over. Your dad is awake. He is in Dr. Cool's lab.

Madeline shook her brother gently.

"Madeline, get off me," Alan murmured.

"Dad is awake," Madeline said.

"Dad woke up?" Alan replied, slowly opening his eyes like a newborn baby.

"Yes. He is in Dr. Cool's lab. But, it is one o' clock already. How do we get to see Dad without being discovered?" Madeline asked.

"Through the air vent," Alan suggested.

"Should we do this now? Or wait until tomorrow morning?" Madeline undecided.

"Madeline, of course we will do it now. Dad is awake. Don't you want to see him first?" Alan said, feeling more energized.

"But –"

"Are you coming or not?" Alan rolled his eyes.

"I want to go but it is dark and -" Madeline hesitated.

"Otherwise I am going without you," Alan said, already putting his shirt on.

"No way! Don't leave me here. Of course I am coming."

"Like mom said, be brave."

The two of them sneaked outside their compartment. They darted left and right in the corridor to make sure they were clear.

"Usually, there will be marines patrolling. Where are they tonight?" Alan wondered.

"I don't know. It will be much easier for us to crawl

into the air duct if they are not here," Madeline said.

They took a corridor to the right where there was a yellow maintenance sign in black text saying:

CAUTION: MAINTENANCE, WORK IN PROGRESS.

"There we are," Alan said.

He quickly kneeled down to remove the grate of the air duct.

Madeline climbed in first. Alan followed and then put the grate back into place.

"It is dark here," Madeline whined.

There was just enough light filtering through the vent and grates for them to see the way.

"That is why I bring this with me." Alan grinned. He turned on the torch function on his phone to illuminate the way.

They ventured in the rectangular tube of the air duct for several minutes.

The long pipes above their head and the leakage of gas were like the hissing of snakes.

They turned right. Headed straight. And then descended down a slope.

The corroded metal on the wall looked like they hadn't been maintained for ages.

"Alan, do you know the way to Dr. Cool's Lab?" Madeline asked impatiently. Her brother should be quite good about his way around here when they were playing hide and seek. It surprised her he took so long to find the way to the lab.

"Over here," a voice muttered from nowhere, making

them jump.

When Alan and Madeline turned around, they could see Andrew at the dead end junction to their right.

"You almost give us a heart attack," Alan said, rolling his eyes.

Then he led Madeline to crawl towards Andrew.

The metal felt cold. Chill invaded their skin.

But, they gritted their teeth to endure all the way.

No matter what, they cannot make any sound.

Not here. Not now.

"What took you guys so long?" Andrew whispered.

"I don't know. Or maybe I just woke up from sleep," Alan made an excuse.

The three of them arranged themselves in position with Madeline in the middle. They peered through the slats of the vent.

An old man in a white lab coat had his back facing them.

He was blocking their sight from seeing their dad.

"Look, Cindy. The general sent the colonial marines to those coordinates to search for those things. Once we learn more about them, we might be able to help your husband," Dr. Cool spoke.

Fear suddenly swept over Cindy.

"No, you can't do that. Ask the General to call the marines to pull back. Those things. There are... there are a lot more of them," Cindy stammered.

"Don't worry. There is nothing the marines can't handle," Dr. Cool said.

"How can I not worry, doctor? Have you tried to remove that thing off Tim's head?" Cindy asked nervously.

Thing? What thing? Madeline was puzzled.

The image of her mother was always a strong character. There is nothing she can't handle.

What is making her mother so anxious now?

It didn't take long before Madeline realized what happened.

She twisted her face in disgust by what she saw as soon as Dr. Cool moved away.

A spidery creature, with eight tri-jointed digits, wrapped itself around their dad's face. Its long tail was latching on his neck like a snake.

"I have tried to remove that, of course." Dr. Cool motioned Cindy to the ground.

There was an uneven hole on the floor. It seemed to be eaten away by some type of acid. Wisp of smoke was hissing from it.

"I have never seen anything like this before. It even melted my clamp." Dr. Cool showed Cindy his medical tool kit.

"What could this be?" Cindy wondered.

"Acid. Highly corrosive acid," Dr. Cool said.

"You mean this thing bleeds acid?" Cindy dropped her mouth opened.

"Apparently, this is the case," Dr. Cool agreed.

Just as they continued with the conversation, a team of marines rushed into the room. Gasping. They were carrying several stretchers with them. Their expression worried.

'They are back. The marines are back!"

"Oh my god…"

The colonists panicked when they saw what the

marines brought back. Their scream echoed in all the corridors of ED-209.

Cindy looked at the marines in fright.

Dread grew inside her like an epidemic.

Like Tim, a marine laid still on the stretcher, with another of those things attached on his face.

"Dr. Cool, we have a situation. Where is the General?" a marine asked.

"The General just left the planet," Dr. Cool said, "I am the second in command for now."

"We…we were ambushed," the marine stammered.

"Where is the rest of the squad?" Dr. Cool asked.

"They…they were outside the complex. There… there are more people on stretchers." The marine gasped.

"How many more?" Dr. Cool pursued. His expression turned serious.

The marine hesitated. He looked at Cindy, and then turned back to Dr. Cool again.

"Tell me."

"Twenty... maybe twenty five. Maybe more on the way," the marine replied.

"How can this even happen? Where is your lieutenant?" Dr. Cool cried.

"Our lieutenant is one of the victims. Everything happened so quickly. The first squad discovered a chamber of egg like things. They walked in and got attacked. Lieutenant and a few other marines tried to save the first group but were ambushed as well."

The children panicked.

Madeline was shaking all over. Tears welled her eyes.

Mommy. What is going on? What is happening to

Daddy? What is happening to everyone?

I want to go home. I want to go back to Earth. I really want to leave.

Didn't you tell me there are no monsters in this world?

Then they heard distant scraping sound from the blackness of the rectangular air duct.

"Guys, did you hear that?" Madeline asked, pointing to the direction where the sound came from.

"What is it?" Alan asked.

"It is just your imagination, Madeline," Andrew said.

"No. It is not. I swear to God I can hear it," Madeline insisted.

"Quiet."

Andrew and Alan could barely hear it at first.

Then the dry scraping sound became louder and more apparent.

The boys swallowed hard.

"Yes. We hear it too," they agreed.

The rattling continued.

Scrape. Scrape. Scrape.

"Alan, lets get out of here. I want to go home. I want to go home," Madeline whined.

"I am afraid we …we can't. This is a dead end here. The only way to get back is to head back to the way where we came in – where the sound comes from," Andrew panicked.

The soft, scratchy sound came closer.

The children scrambled away.

They kept crawling back until their back hit a cold metal plate.

It was a dead end.

Madeline squeezed between the boys.

Her heart was pounding fast.

She looked at the Alan. His body tensed. Sweat was raining down his forehead.

"Please –" Madeline uttered in a low, choked voice. " Please – go away!"

No reply.

She stared into blackness, but could see nothing.

Scrape. Scrape. Scrape.

The sound is so close that it seemed like it is right in front of them.

I will never play hide and seek in the air duct anymore. I will never do that anymore. But, right now, I need to be brave.

"Alan."

No reply.

"Andrew."

No reply.

"Stop kidding around. Not now!"

Madeline's hand touched something cold. It felt like a phone – Alan's phone.

Be brave. Face it. Madeline told herself.

She switched on the torch function from the phone to illuminate the air duct.

All of a sudden, something leaped and wrapped around her face.

The next thing she heard was her own scream.

PART 5

33

"Sadly, by the time we found the children in the air duct, it was too late." Dr. Cool sighed.

"So, where is everyone? Why did you evacuate ED-209?" I asked.

Just when Dr. Cool was about to reveal what happened, a transmission from the colonial marines interrupted our conversation.

"Cap…Captain Eva, do…do you copy?"

Static filled the voice.

"Eva here. What is the situation down there?" Eva turned on her microphone and asked.

"We … we have found the colonists. But - "

"But what?"

"But they … they have cocooned into…into some kind of egg… reptile egg."

My heart was racing.

I gazed at the ovoid, leathery egg on the table, with four petal-like lips opened.

Is that what the marines are seeing too? Or is it something else?

"Then get them out of here and regroup with us," Eva commanded.

"No. We...we tried. But...but we can't get them out of here."

"Why not? Speak louder. I cannot hear you," Eva demanded.

"Because they became part of the egg themselves."

***

The colonist moaned in pain as the marines tried one last time to separate him from the egg.

"Captain, this...this is unreal. How can this be possible?" The marine twisted his face in disgust. He exchanged a puzzled look with Captain Ian, who looked blank.

Then they heard Eva from the radio.

"Fall back," Eva said.

"What about the colonists?" Ian asked.

"Fall back and regroup. Situation changes," Eva commanded.

"But, we just found the colonists. This is a rescue mission," Tommy protested.

"This is an order," Eva insisted.

"You heard the commander?" Captain Ian asked Tommy.

The marines slowly retreated.

The corridor was dark.

The basement of the atmospheric processing unit was like a labyrinth.

They turned one corner after another. Everywhere looked almost identical.

Dim, filtered light escaped from the slats of the corroded fans.

Broken cables were left hanging with arcs and sparks.

Long gas pipes hissed like venomous pythons.

Occasionally, the leakage gas blocked their sight.

The rumbling sound of the machine filled the background.

Tommy and Ian wondered how the colonists worked in this kind of environment. This place seemed like it has not been maintained for a century.

Soon, they arrived at a new area with a high ceiling.

"Captain, we haven't been to this place before, right?" Nguyen asked.

"I have no idea," Ian replied.

"We have been searching for the service elevator for a while now," Roger complained.

"Well, we are just heading back where we came from. The elevator can't just disappear into thin air right?" Ian assured. "Keep looking."

Paris stepped on something that made a soft, squelching sound.

He lifted his boot and illuminated it with his shoulder lamp.

Strands of slime stretched like spider web between his boot and the ground.

"What is that?" Paris narrowed his eyes.

The others swallowed hard.

No one spoke a single word.

A few drops of mucus like substances dripped from the ceiling onto Paris's vest.

It was sticky, like the slime he stepped on the floor.

Slowly, Paris raised his head up.

Circles of spotlight from his shoulder lamp danced at the ceiling.

"Guys, over here," Paris shared his discovery.

The marines shone their lamps around.

"What the – "

They discovered the ceiling was severely damaged. Panels of the air duct were down. Water pipes tattered. Black resin spread everywhere.

The sound of water dribble from a ruptured channel sang in the background.

BEEP, BEEP, BEEP.

Suddenly, the motion tracker in Tommy's hand sprang into life.

Something isn't right.

"Uh, Captain…" Tommy looked at the reading.

"Talk to me, Tommy," Captain Ian asked.

"Movements," Tommy exclaimed. His eyes focused on the bright display. Multiple signatures appeared on screen.

"They…they are everywhere," Tommy choked.

Nguyen darted left and right, up and down.

"I can't see anything, man," Nguyen disagreed.

"Sol, are you seeing anything? Check the corners," Roger asked.

"Nothing back here." Sol shrugged.

"Tommy, are you sure you are reading this right?" Paris challenged.

"I swear to God they are here! They are right here!" Tommy insisted.

Captain Ian swung his pulse rifle in an arc, shining

light into the shadow.

BEEP, BEEP, BEEP.

"Ten meters."

The sound intensity of the motion detector increased.

Tommy could hear his own breathing.

His hands trembled.

His heart was pounding in fear.

Although he had been trained as a colonial marine, the trainings were merely stimulations. They are nothing compared to real life.

Nothing like this at all.

BEEP, BEEP, BEEP.

"Five meters."

"Four."

34

A shrill scream of horror filled the room, loud enough to be heard over the background sound of the machines

When the marines turned around, they saw Roger being hauled upward, desperately attempting to kick free. An unusual long, segmented, blade-tipped tail wrapped around his waist.

The marines were caught by surprise.

Their flickering, spotlights danced around the Roger, trying to get a glimpse of what caught their companion.

"What the –"

Without warning, the tail pulled Roger into the shadow and slip away.

"Help!!!!!"

All that was left of Roger was a distant scream of despair, echoing away.

"No!" Paris and Nguyen lost their temper.

They aimed at the shadow above them and began to open fire.

"Cease fire!" Ian roared. "You could have killed Roger."

"Captain, didn't you see what happened?" Paris cried breathlessly, pointing at the shadow.

"That thing … it just took him away… before our eyes," Nguyen said with a Vietnamese accent.

Fear and doubt clouded the marines.

They began to question their captain's ability to lead…

"Movement!" Tommy shouted again.

HISS, HISS, HISS.

Inhuman hisses echoed in the corridor where the marines came in.

Louder and louder each passing second.

Shadows were moving behind the machines, the grates and vents.

"We need to leave," Ian ordered.

"But what about the service elevator?" Nguyen contested.

"We need to leave now! Move. We will find another way."

***

Alex gazed impatiently at his watch.

He began to worry.

The captain had been gone for a very long time now.

Had something gone wrong?

But the captain ordered them to stay and guard the elevator until they returned…

Going down to find the captain would be disobeying his order.

But, they can't stand here forever either. Eva is waiting

for them in the complex.

"I envy Dante and Virgil," William, one of the marines, said.

"Why do you say so?" Benjamin asked. He wore a cross necklace around his neck.

"Because they are probably sleeping in the crawler right now," William replied.

"I would probably be worrying about the captain and his team down there right now more than those two sleeping in the crawler," Benjamin said, touching his cross, for good luck.

"Why is that? Our captain is a pretty tough guy." William arched an eyebrow.

"Check the watch. They have gone for a very long time," Benjamin said.

Alex looked at the marines.

He wished he could contact the captain right now. But, some type of electromagnetic shielding blocked their communication.

Isn't that brilliant!

"Lieutenant, should we go and check it out?" Russell suggested.

Alex gazed at his watch again. It had been three hours. There might be a lot of colonists down there. But, it wouldn't take their captain that long to bring them up. Not with Ian's ability.

Just as Alex authorized the team, the elevator they were guarding suddenly sprang into life.

There was just enough light filtered from the vents so they could see the elevator display.

"Whoa, looks like they are finally back." William

yawned, stretching.

"Yeah, finally," Alex uttered a long sigh of relieve.

The elevator rumbled and hummed as it continued to ascend.

A strange odor invaded their nostrils.

The scent grew much stronger when the elevator was about to arrive.

"That is pure …disgusting," William complained, trying to come up with a word to suit.

Alex ignored the scent. He stood close to the door, couldn't wait to be the first one to greet his comrade.

DING

The elevator arrived.

It rumbled and clattered as the door slowly slid opened.

"Captain, I am glad you finally - "

Alex was staring at an abyss.

There was no captain. No marines.

A tall humanoid figure emerged from the darkness of the elevator, towering over him.

Alex slowly tilted his head.

He could feel drops of blood drip from his nose.

Just as he was about to turn around, the creature lunged for his throat.

The next thing he heard was his own scream.

35

The familiar sound of the pulsing rifle gunfire pierced through the air.

"What the –" Ian and his squad were caught out by surprise.

The marines paused and listened.

The gunfire lasted for a few minutes and died.

"Wh-who is firing?" Tommy asked.

"It came from upstairs. It must be from Alex and his team. They must be in trouble," Ian assured.

Then he shouted over the radio.

"Alex, do you copy?"

No reply.

"This is Captain Ian, do you copy?"

Still no reply.

"First it is Roger. Now, it is the marines upstairs. I have a bad feeling that our mission is a big mistake. The company didn't tell us what we are supposed to know," Nguyen spoke.

"Captain, do you know what are we dealing with?" Paris arched an eyebrow.

"Captain. All we were briefed was to ensure Eva's safety," Nguyen added. "No one mentioned anything about what actually happened in ED-209. Why are those cocooned colonists morphing in eggs? What was that thing that grabbed Roger? What is attacking us?"

"You asked too many questions, comrade. As marines, we never question the company. We just follow orders. Right now, my order for you is to find a way back to the surface and regroup with the rest of the team," Ian commanded.

BEEP, BEEP, BEEP.

The motion sensor vibrated.

"Guys…those things… whatever they are…they are behind us again. We don't have time to talk. We have to leave," Tommy stammered.

"You hear that comrade? Let's get moving."

***

Another hour passed, and we still hadn't heard back from the marines.

I gazed at Hiroyuki with that spider like creature latched on his face.

It gave me a shiver.

We should have listened to Dr. Cool and never came to this planet.

Now, the marines disappeared. Hiroyuki is in trouble. Everyone in this room is panicked.

But, we cannot abandon the marines on this planet.

I am not sure about the others. But, I just couldn't do it.

Too many things happened since we landed.

Too many unexpected things happened…

Things that aren't supposed to be real…

"We can't stay here and wait for the marines forever," Molly suggested.

"There is a debris storm in our route back to Earth right now. The satellites are down. If even one of those debris hit our ship, we will be lost in space forever. No one will come to rescue us," Eva argued.

Dr. Cool coughed. But, he said nothing.

"Look at Hiroyuki. If we never came to this planet, and to this room, he would never have had this… disgusting thing on this face. We should hurry up and bring him back to Earth for treatment," Karen snapped.

"I am afraid this is not possible. We have to wait for the marines before anything can happen," Eva refused.

"Captain Eva, you promised us to only stay here for a while," Peter whined.

Eva ignored him.

She walked over to Dr. Cool.

"You know what is happening, right?" Eva asked coldly.

But, Dr. Cool shrugged.

"It is your work. It is your lab. It is your egg," Eva scolded.

We looked at Dr. Cool, waiting for an answer.

Just as the doctor about to reply, a transmission from Captain Ian made everyone freeze.

36

"Thanks God we can finally connect." Ian uttered a long sigh of relieve.

"Captain Ian, what is your position right now?" Eva asked.

"We don't know. We are somewhere in the basement of the atmospheric processing unit."

"Is everyone all right? Hang in there. We are coming," Eva said.

"Please. Don't come."

"Why?"

"We lost Roger… Something hideous got him. It lifted him up and pulled into the vent," Ian apologized.

"Did you see what is it?"

"Unfortunately, we didn't. It was too fast. All we could see were moving shadows."

What could possibly drag Roger away from a group of armed marines?

"We heard gunfire from the upper level. They must have got Alex and his team too!" Tommy cried. We could hear panic fill his voice.

"Tommy, Sol, are you okay?" we asked.

"It is like a labyrinth down here," Sol said.

"Can't you follow the original way you came from?" Peter queried.

"No way man! Those creatures blocked us. We can detect them. We can hear them hissing. But, we couldn't see them," Tommy snapped.

"Captain Eva, we have exhausted our options. I am afraid you might have to leave without us…" Ian said reluctantly.

"Captain, I respect you. I cannot believe you would say that!"

The marines protested in the background.

"Marines, I want you to stay calm," Eva said. "If we are to leave, we leave together as a team."

"Captain Ian, there is actually another way that can lead you back without going back to the surface," Dr. Cool suggested.

"What do you mean?"

Everyone turned to the doctor.

"There is a tunnel underneath this building. It connects with all the atmospheric processing units in ED-209. They were for maintenance workers to travel to and from the atmospheric processing units without being exposed to the catastrophic storms above ground," Dr. Cool said.

"Ian, give us your location," Eva requested.

"Just a moment." Ian pressed a few buttons on a device mounted on his gauntlet.

"Great. Marines, hang in there. Stay in your position. I am going down to meet you," Eva promised.

She wasted no time to arm herself.

"Wait…I will go with you," I volunteered.

"No. It is too dangerous," Eva rejected.

"I must come. It is too dangerous for you to go alone. I will watch your back," I insisted.

Peter pulled my sleeves. Worried filled his eyes.

"Sol and Tommy are our peers. I must go," I explained to Peter.

Peter hesitated.

"I don't want you to go," Peter said in a low voice.

"Don't worry. It is going to be okay. I will be back, and we will leave together," I said.

Slowly, Peter let go.

"You promise you will be back?"

"I promise. Stay with Dr. Cool and give us support."

Then we fist-bumped each other to promise each other to meet again.

37

Eva and I gasped.

Our boots were thudding hard as we descended the metal grates of the stairwell.

The marines were miles away. It would certainly take us hours to reach them on foot.

"Whatever happens, stay close to me. It will be dark in the tunnel, use these flares to mark the way," Eva said and shoved the flares box to me.

A few minutes later, we arrived at the basement.

The power was down.

The place was so dark that we could barely see our fingers.

Eva ignited one of the flares. She tossed it at a distance to illuminate the place.

A heavy metal door with a hatch appeared in sight. It was worn and corroded. Black and yellow strips were adhered on the edges. There was a sign embossed on the center labeled: KEEP OUT. AUTHORISED PERSONNEL ONLY.

"Dr. Cool, we are at the basement," Eva spoke over

the radio.

"Good. You should see a metal door. Proceed through the door and head straight," Dr. Cool said.

Eva turned the hatch.

The door was heavy.

The two of us pushed the creaking door open with all our strength.

"I hate that terrible creaking sound," I complained.

"I bet there are a lot more doors like this in the tunnel," Eva said.

We ventured through the tunnel and slammed the metal door behind us.

Then we turned on our shoulder lamp. Spots of light darted left and right in the enormous mouth of the concrete tunnel. The ceiling and wall were stained. I could clearly hear water dripping from the poorly sealed pipe joints.

This place is nightmarish.

It is nowhere close to what Dr. Kim described to us when she recruited us to terraform Zeptune.

I can't imagine any colonists would like to work in this type of place.

Except for slaves.

Wait a minute, didn't Mom and Dad leave me to terraform other planets as well?

Mom... Dad…

Why did you leave me for a place like this?

I am missing you already…

"Wait."

All of a sudden, Eva roared and interrupted my thoughts.

"Eva, what is it?" I asked.

Eva tilted her spotlight that danced at the top of the high ceiling.

I could see dark, resinous substance latching on the surface of the concrete like fungus.

Some of the resin hardened. Others dripped like glue.

Some parts appeared to be opaque. Other parts were darkened black and gray.

The peculiar things looked like some uniform menace patterns of chitin and sharp tails on the wall.

Both of us couldn't take our eyes off our discovery.

"Eva, have … have you seen anything like this before?" I asked.

"No. I haven't. First time," Eva whispered. "But I know someone might have an idea."

38

"Dr. Cool, where are you going?" Peter panicked when Dr. Cool began to pack up.

The doctor hurried to a workbench. He retrieved some samples and shoved it in a metal case.

"Silly boy, of course, I am leaving." Dr. Cool grinned.

"Leaving? But aren't we waiting for Eva and Nova?" Peter asked.

"Don't worry. They are in my labyrinth. They won't be back," Dr. Cool said.

"What do you mean they won't be back?" Peter was confused.

"I think you have been mistaken. My order is to research on the Trinomorph project and bring back a sample for the General. I have no interest in helping you or them." Dr. Cool laughed.

"Trinomorph?" Molly frowned.

"Yes. Trinomorph. It is for the company's bio-weapon division. That creature latching on your friend's face is merely the infancy stage of a Trinomorph. It leaves behind a tumor in his chest cavity that changes his cells inside his body. In a few hours or so, a hideous creature will grow in your friend's body. It will hatch, granting him a horrible, painful death." Dr. Cool pointed at the poor, motionless Hiroyuki lying on the floor.

"This poor boy risked his life saving yours," Karen challenged.

"Oh really? This poor boy messed up my whole plan. I was on my way back to the interstellar cruiser ST-132 to report my spectacular findings after escaping this rotten place. Unfortunately, I crash landed onto Quir. But the rescue teams were on their way. My ship detected yours heading towards Ed-209. That was why I sent a SOS signal to warn you to stay away. We cannot afford to let anyone find out what happened in ED-209," Dr. Cool revealed.

Peter, Karen and Molly were shocked by the truth.

Dr. Cool knew everything from the beginning…

"Remember, I did warn you not to come. But, your captain refused to listen. All she cares about is to find out about her past. That is why she came back. Ultimately, it is Eva you should blame. None of this would have happened if she didn't make this reckless, impulsive decision coming back to ED-209," Dr. Cool mocked.

He cautiously moved towards the exit of the building.

"You are a doctor. You are supposed to save life," Molly said.

"I am saving it already," Dr. Cool said as he motioned the kids to a specimen in his shiny, metal case.

"You are evil."

"Whatever you say, kids. I am missing all of you already," Dr. Cool said and exited the lab.

Peter was angry and frightened.

They had never been put in this type of situation before.

In St. George Orphan School, Miss O' Connor planned everything for them. There were only a few minor decisions they needed to make. Their only big decision they had ever made was to go to space.

"I... I am going down there to find Nova," Peter insisted.

"No. Don't. Didn't you hear what the mad doctor said? It is a labyrinth down there." Molly held Peter by the arm.

"It is too dangerous. Eva took weapons with her. Do you know even how to fire a gun?" Karen rejected.

"No. I don't. But, if I don't warn my sister, she will definitely die down there!" Peter argued. "They won't be that far ahead of me."

"Peter, I say no! Stay where you are. If Eva and Nova come back and find out we are not here, they will be very anxious," Molly said shrilly.

"But -"

Just as Peter was about to speak again, a sudden scream from the corridor tore the air.

"Wh- what was that?" Karen stammered, feeling a sudden chill.

"I... I don't know." Peter swallowed hard.

The three of them huddled together underneath a bench just enough to hide.

Shivering. Shaking. Panicking.

The scream died off, overheard by an inhuman hiss.

Peter focused on the entrance.

His heart pounded so fast that it almost skipped a beat.

Whatever this thing is, it must have gotten Dr. Cool...

HISS, HISS, HISS.

The hissing came closer and louder.

What is it? What could it be?

He looked at Molly and Karen, who sandwiched him in between.

They covered their face with both hands.

No one spoke a single word.

HISS, HISS, HISS.

When Peter turned to the entrance again, he saw a hideous shadow slither slowly at the entrance of the lab.

39

"Hello? Dr. Cool. This is Eva speaking. If you hear me, please pick up my call," Eva tried one last time to make contact with the doctor, but no one was picking up from the end.

"Strange, we just spoke a moment ago. Why did we lose contact all of a sudden?" I was puzzled.

"I know I shouldn't be relying on him. He cannot be trusted," Eva complained.

"Eva, should we go in?"

"What choice do we have?"

Eva ignited another flare and threw it at the corner of the tunnel.

I stared at the bright, sparkling flare on the ground. This is our only indicator to go back where we came from.

"How long do we have till the flares extinguish?" I asked.

"Five hours," Eva replied. "That is what we have to find the marines and get out of here."

We moved cautiously inside the tunnel.

Both sides of the wall were like some giant ribcage of an enormous worm that branched out into the abyss.

Yellow working light stands were left abandoned on the floor.

The dark, resinous substance engulfed everything in its path. Every door, every room, every duct, every machine was threaded by some kind of branch like web.

We pressed on.

The sound of water dripping sang in my ears.

It was so clear.

Leakage gas from pipes almost made it impossible to see.

A moment later, we arrived at a slope.

We followed it and curved downwards to a lower chamber.

Stack of generators were humming loudly behind the flickering blue light. They almost gave me an illusion of some kind of monsters moaning in the background.

"Careful, Nova, this chamber is flooded," Eva warned.

"Cold…cold," I complained. "The water level rose up to my knee."

"Stay sharp. Remember, we are on our own," Eva reminded.

I followed Eva closely.

The water damaged almost everything in the chamber.

I checked my surrounding. The screen of a working laptop caught the corner of my eyes. I looked at it out of curiosity. There was an email addressed to Dr. Cool.

"Eva, come and have a look," I said.

DATE: 11 MAY 2150

Dr. Cool, two more scheduled shuttles are
scheduled to arrive here in a few months to
repopulate ED-209. This time, the passengers
are orphans. No one will know their existence. They will be perfect specimens for
your experiment. The two terraformers, Tim
Shaun and Cindy Shaun, are very close to dis-
covering what happened to the missing terraformers. Should we do something about them?

Orphans? Are they referring to us? What does this
have to do with Dr. Cool? What experiments are they
conducting?

I recalled Dr. Cool's story of Tim and Cindy and the
ordeal the Shaun family had been through.

I continued to read.

Oh wait, this one is from Dr. Cool.

DATE: 18 June 2150

General, I am writing to you in case I don't
make it back to the interstellar cruiser
alive. The chemical, TERA-102100X.141, emitted from Fornax A, is extremely unstable
under ambient temperature. It infested several of our atmospheric processing units with
black mold. Several terraformers and maintenance workers working there were exposed.
The chemical rewrites their DNA. They become
extremely aggressive and seemingly mindless
as they attack any living thing in sight. The
colonial marines are already investigating
the missing colonists. If they reached the
labyrinth, I fear they will discover my secret lab, or worse, my pet …

The email ended.

I turned to Eva, who was as stunned as I was. The strange doctor is truly unpredictable.

Are there other labs in the labyrinth? What pet is Dr. Cool referring to? What is this chemical TERA-102100X.141 from Fornax A?

I focused on the dark, resinous substance.

Is Dr. Cool referring to this? Is this the chemical from Fornax A black hole?

Questions were circling around my head like a carousel.

"What is Dr. Cool doing?" Eva murmured.

She began to search the room for more evidence.

She scrambled over a pile of wet paper on a tray. Some of them were showing the complex floorplan of the place. Some were showing schematics and sketches of humanoid creatures with elongated heads.

"This is insane. This is criminal. They are using colonists for some type of experiment. We might be part of his plan already."

"Eva, we should continue to find the marines and get out of here before the flares extinguish," I suggested.

"Yeah. You are right. We should press on," Eva replied, but couldn't take her eyes off the chamber.

We got back on track.

Our shoulder headlamps darted left and right.

Suddenly, I saw something...

I vaguely saw the tangled cables behind generators slither in flickering blue light.

"What the?" I exclaimed, focusing my circle of spotlight to the generators.

"What is it?" Eva asked.

"I...I think I saw something just move." I pointed to the cables.

Step by step, Eva approached with caution.

Then she stopped halfway.

At first, we though we both had an illusion.

But, this time Eva saw it too.

The creature cleverly clung itself in the labyrinthine machinery that we thought was part of the generator.

The creature slithered slowly. Its body remained unseen. The only part exposed was its blackish, curved, elongated head so wet that we almost saw our reflection.

Has the creature discovered us? Can it hear us? Can it smell us? More importantly, how smart is it?

It won't be long until we find out...

"Back away slowly," Eva instructed me. She lifted her pulse rifle and aimed at the creature.

Breathing deeply.

The blue light flickered.

I couldn't take my eyes off the creature.

I wanted to know exactly where it is any moment.

I don't want to guess where it goes if it disappears.

Suddenly, something wet my left shoulder.

I thought it was the dripping water at first.

But, I was wrong.

I reached out and my fingers were covered with strands of thick, slimy substance.

Yuck....

It was no water...it was some kind of salvia.

The dripping quickened.

Slowly, I tilted my head.

Then I saw it in my juddering beam of spotlight.

It has been stalking us all along...

The blackish creature hung upside down. It had an elongated head protected by a large crest. Saliva was dripping vigorously from its fangs. Its hooded torso was one giant ribcage. With neither arms nor legs, it slithered with its unusual long spiky tail like a snake.

My body was shaking.

My heart was pounding so fast that it almost skipped

a beat.

"Ev –"

My mind went blank.

I tried to speak but no sound came out.

Then I felt something slowly wrapping around my legs and body.

The creature hissed.

"Noooooooo."

Before Eva realized, I was pulled into the darkness of the air duct above me.

The next thing I heard was my scream.

PART 6

41

W here am I?

I could hear distant human voices.

Screaming. Sobbing. Begging.

My body felt weak.

The smell was… unbearable.

I tried to open my eyes. But, something slimy and wet stopped me.

I blinked a few times and reopened them again.

I realized I was attached to the chamber wall with thick strands of translucent, web like resin, a few meters above ground.

Huh?

I tried to move my arms and legs, but the resin was simply too adhesive.

My back was glued to the wall.

The only part I could move was my head.

"Help!" I shrieked at the top of my lungs.

"Help?"

A familiar, hoarse voice mocked.

"Who is that?" I asked.

I drifted my attention to the source of the voice behind the flickering blue light.

Then, I saw Dr. Cool.

He had the same fate as me.

I focused on the figures behind him.

My heart was racing.

Oh my god!

They were the colonists and the marines.

One by one, they were cocooned along an uneven path from the wall, all the way up to the ceiling.

I tilted my head to follow the path.

To my horror, I saw bloated, swollen, mutilated bodies hung upside down.

Some of them were still breathing.

42

A high-pitched scream interrupted Eva's thoughts.

She couldn't believe the creature stole Nova right before her eyes.

No. I can't let this happen again. I can't!

She began to recall distant memories…the memories of a brutal creature smuggled into her ship from ED-209 and slaughtered her entire crew, which eventually forced her to blow up the ship before it reached Earth.

The memories of her not being able to save any of her crew haunted her every night…

Even though it was eighty years ago.

That is why she is back.

She wanted to find out about the origin of the creature and prove to the company that it exists.

She did not blow up the ship for no reason.

The screaming continues…

This time it is louder.

It sounded just like her daughter screaming for her to come back.

Mom. I came first in class. I want to show you the

award Mrs. O'Donnell gave me in front of the whole class. Where are you?

Mom. I am picking which university to go to. Can you give me some advice?

Mom. Today is my graduation day. Everyone is taking photos with their parents. Where are you?

Mom. I feel so sad. Leon left me. Where are you?

Eva wiped her tears away.

I will save you Nova.

I will get you out of here alive.

I promise.

43

"Welcome to the hive cluster." Dr. Cool uttered a horrible laugh.

I screamed and screamed.

The abominations were moaning... making horrible noises ... like a goose.

When I lowered my head, I could see several turkey like creatures with long necks. They had no eyes, no nose, but a jaw filled with human like teeth. Their body was blood stained like newborn babies after birth.

One of them quacked at me vigorously.

The others followed.

When I looked closely, they ... they seemed to be chewing some type of intestine...

"Help!!!!!!!"

"Feast on her and grow." Dr. Cool grinned.

Burst of fire showered onto the creatures below my feet.

The creatures shrieked in pain and collapsed.

I turned my attention to the sound of fire.

I saw a figure standing in the entrance of the chamber.

"Eva!" I cried.

"Nova, thank God I finally find you. All your friends are waiting for you. Are you all right?" Eva said.

She hurried to me and removed me from the strands of webbing by force.

In the midst of freeing me, I saw a tall shadow emerging from behind Eva.

"Eva, behind you!" I shouted as the shadow charged toward her.

Without thinking, Eva rolled back, aimed and pulled the trigger.

Whatever that creature is, its body blew into fragments.

Acidic blood spattered and burned everywhere and onto Dr. Cool's face.

Dr. Cool screamed in pain as the acid ate away part of his skin.

"Don't be so naive. Do you think you can get out of here alive?" Dr. Cool growled.

Eva freed me.

She turned to the mad doctor just as we were about to leave.

"Free me. Please. You will need my help," Dr. Cool pleaded. "It is a labyrinth down here. It is designed to be like his. It is designed by me."

"Doctor, why are you doing this?" Eva asked coldly.

"We were under direct order from the General to study captive Trinomorph specimens – the creatures you just killed. We do that to study the creature's behavior with the intention to be able to control them as weapons in the space race," Dr. Cool explained.

"I know that. We saw it on one of your labs right after you deserted us in the tunnel," Eva replied coldly. "Tell me, what have you found?"

"These creatures don't consider themselves as individuals. Pain. Fatigue. Nothing mitigates their aggression to kill, cocoon victims to ensure the survival of their species. They have some kind of hive mind," Dr. Cool shared his findings.

"Hive mind?" Eva frowned.

I glanced at my surrounding.

Dr. Cool is right. The ambience in this place resembled some type of hive to a degree.

"Yes. Hive mind. Collective intelligence. Or swarm intelligence. These creatures do not think like individuals. They think like a colony of honeybees. We were trying to exploit their hive mind behavior and attempt to replicate that to control them. But, we failed. They outsmarted us," Dr. Cool continued.

"Tell me about chemical TERA-102100X.141?" Eva pursued.

"Chemical TERA-102100X.141 is what started all this. These horrifying creatures you saw are not indigenous in ED-209. They are the result of living things exposed to Chemical TERA-102100X.141 – an virulent mutagenic pathogen found on rocks orbiting black hole Fornax A," Dr. Cool said.

"Do you mean these monsters are created from some unknown pathogen from rocks deorbited Fornax A and somehow landed on ED209?" I guessed. "But, nothing escapes a black hole."

"Nothing, but dark matter," Dr. Cool corrected.

"Dark matter?" I was confused.

"Unlike normal matter, some dark matter can escape a black hole, no matter what size the black hole and no matter how close the dark matter is to the black hole. It seems like maybe there exist some types of intelligence human yet to understand. Our discovery of chemical TERA-102100X.141 is only a tiny piece of puzzle to that," Dr. Cool speculated.

An inhuman roar from a distance sent a shiver down our spines.

The ground began to tremble.

It felt like something big is coming.

"Are you finally ready to get me out of here?" Dr. Cool asked impatiently.

"Show us the way out of here."

Eva and I blindly followed Dr. Cool.

We turned corners after corners.

Soon, we lost direction.

The leaked gas from broken gas pipes blew in our face.

Constant gas leak sound whistled in our ears.

We could barely see anything ahead of us.

All we felt was warm and humid.

"This way," Dr. Cool said.

But, his voiced seemed miles away.

Crazy doctor. Why you are running so fast all of a sudden?

Eva and I hurried after him breathlessly.

We exited the last curtain of mist.

Then everything was dark again.

A blue beacon flickered in the dark background every few seconds.

I tried to locate Dr. Cool, but he was gone.

Yes. Gone again.

He tricked us into saving him and deserted us.

We shouldn't have trusted him to lead us out of this place.

Before we took another step, both of us were stopped by some strange, soft sucking noise.

It sounded familiar.

"Don't move," Eva whispered. Her expression solemn like the first time we met. Her eyes wide open.

What is going on?

In the midst of the flickering blue light, I saw something familiar...

I saw an ovoid, brown-black, leathery object, with four petal-like lips at the top.

No. Not one. But dozens and dozens of them!

They looked exactly like the egg we saw in Dr. Cool's lab!

Except, they looked bigger... they are up to my waist.

Tendril-like roots spread from its base.

Pulsing.

A wet, squishing sound to my right drew my attention.

Strings of mucus hanging from the petal like lips split apart.

The two of us stood like statues.

What already happened to Hiroyuki flashback in our minds.

We were trapped.

Why are there so many eggs in here?

No. This is not the question.

The real question should be: who laid these eggs?

The wet sucking sound drew our attention again.

Slowly, our eyes followed the source of the sound.

An enormous, slimy worm-like structure was dangling in mid-air.

Wriggling. Squirming.

"Is…is it a worm?" I stammered.

The structure expanded and contracted. It uttered a disgusting, squish sound. Then an egg is spilled out, covered by slim and strands of mucus.

Yuck!

"It…it is not a worm. It looks more like some kind of ovipositor to me," Eva replied softly.

A loud, inhuman hiss sent a chill down our spines.

When we tilted our head, a giant creature revealed itself from shadow of darkness.

The creature looked like it was born for killing. It stood at least fifteen meters in height. It had no eyes and nose, but an armored skull that resembled a crest. A row of blunted spikes filled with pulsing blood vessels ran down its elongated head. Its giant bat-like membrane wings opened up, revealing its massive insect arms and legs. Its lower torso was connecting to the ovipositor.

It must be responsible for laying those eggs.

It must be the Queen.

The Queen towered above us like a skyscraper.

It swiped its tail left and right.

Snarling.

Clearly, it was not welcoming us as guests.

My eyes locked on it.

I swallowed hard.

Sweat was running down my forehead like rain.

We waited.

Surprisingly, the creature did not attack us.

"Nova, stand behind me. Slowly. One step at a time," Eva said quietly.

Eva lifted her pulse rifle slowly and aimed it at the egg next to me.

Without warning, she pulled the trigger and the egg exploded into pieces.

The Queen roared.

Shadows behind her began to move.

Eva lost her cool.

She let loose with battle cry and sent volleys of bullets into the eggs and shadows.

All of a sudden, the chamber was filling with dying inhuman cries.

Eva clenched her teeth.

She shoots and shoots and shoots.

The remains of the Trinomorph and egg sac flew everywhere.

The number on the LED counter was showing her ammo dropped like a rocket.

"Die, you wretched creature!" Eva shrieked.

She strafed a grenade from her pulse rifle straight into the ovipositor.

The egg sack exploded instantly, sending yellow liquid spilling everywhere.

She reloaded and sent another grenade to a generator.

BANG!

The machines behind hordes of Trinomorph exploded.

Within seconds, the whole place was surrounded by a sea of fire.

The Queen hissed.

"Eva, let's go!" I yelled.

The two of us turned around.

We scrambled our way aimlessly through the corridors.

Falling. Getting back up again. Gasping.

We turned one corner after another.

The inhuman shrieks were behind us.

They echoed in the labyrinth of corridors.

There is no time to think.

There is no time to stop.

We must get out of here.

We will regroup with the crew and leave this place.

We will make it.

We definitely will.

46

Peter stood at the ram of the drop ship, searching the horizontal with a pair of binoculars.

He checked his watch impatiently every two seconds.

His gripped the cross in his pocket with his right hand.

Praying.

Eva, please, you have to find Nova. You have to find her and get her out of here.

"Peter, come back inside. It is too stormy," Dr. Kim gestured at the boy, shouting at the top of her lungs.

But the wind howled louder.

Wind-driven grit made the visibility so low they he could hardly see anything.

General Muesel came over and stood beside Peter.

"We are leaving in ten minutes," General Muesel announced coldly.

The General tapped his hand on Peter's shoulder, signaling him to put the binoculars away and prepare to leave.

"General Muesel, Eva is already searching for Nova. I believe she will find her. I am not leaving without my sister!" Peter protested.

"This is not a choice. This is an order. You must put your personal feelings aside. Look at your friends." General Muesel motioned him to inside the dropship.

He saw Molly and Karen were shaking. Sol and Tommy were wounded, clenching their teeth in pain.

Then he saw Hiroyuki San, who had that thing wrapped around his neck.

"Peter, you must understand. Dr. Kim and I risked our lives to come here and save you and your crew. It is by sheer luck we found you and the others. If we don't take Hiroyuki to the medical bay immediately, I fear for his life. I am sure your sister will understand this," General Muesel said.

Peter's eyes welled with tears.

His last words with Nova crashed in his mind like waves.

"I don't want you to go."

"Don't worry. It is going to be okay. I will be back and we will leave together."

"You promise you will be back?"

"I promise. Stay with Dr. Cool and give us support."

Nova, I should have gone with you. We shouldn't have separated in the first place. Peter sobbed.

Suddenly, he saw something staggering from a distance.

Peter raised his pair of binoculars again.

He zoomed in and saw two familiar faces.

It was Eva and Nova.

Without thinking, Peter raced down the ram.

"Hey, Peter, what are you doing? We are leaving."

Everyone in the dropship shouted.

Peter ran and ran, leaving the voice of the others behind.

Gust of wind and grit paddled his face.

He clenched his teeth and ignored the pain.

Then he saw Eva appeared from the horizon of the slope first, followed by Nova.

They must have seen him too.

"Nova, over here!" Peter cried, waving at them as if he had missed them for centuries.

Then he felt the ground rumble.

The noise was small at first but it grew louder and louder by the second.

Something is wrong.

Instead of seeing them waved back, he saw panic in their eyes.

They gestured him to go away.

47

"GO! GO! GO!"

Eva didn't even bother to greet Peter.

She did not want Peter to see the horror behind them.

She grabbed him by the arm and sped to the drop-ship.

I didn't look back either.

I felt like I was in the final stage of a marathon.

Everything around me became flying color.

I promised myself not to stop.

The ram of the dropship is my goal.

So, I ran and ran and ran.

My heart beat frantically.

The cold air invaded my throat and lung as I inhaled deeper, faster.

Pain shot through my ankle to knee.

I can do nothing except clenching my teeth to endure.

I swung my sweaty fists forward to make me go faster.

Gasping.

The ram of the dropship grew bigger and bigger in sight.

Yes. We are there.

We are almost there.

I saw the familiar face of General Muesel and Dr. Kim.

Molly and Karen were right beside them.

Everyone was gesturing at us to hurry.

The ground continued to rumble.

An inhuman growl from behind us grew louder.

We destroyed their hive.

They were not going to let us leave.

Eva threw Peter onto the ram first.

She hopped in from behind.

Good. They made it.

I am almost there.

Only a couple of meters and I will be out of this place.

Whoa! Noooooo!

A rocked tripped me.

I staggered for a second, but I lost my balance.

My whole body twirled and jerked.

Everything blurred.

Then I felt the pain.

Ouch!

My clothes were torn. My skin reddened.

"No. General, you can't do this to her," Peter shrieked.

Before I realized what was happening, the ram began to close.

Oh nooooooo.

They decided to leave me behind…

All of a sudden, my hope of escaping shattered like broken glass on the floor.

I tilted my head and saw the others defying the general's decision.

But, it was too late.

I could feel the creatures' hot breath pressed against my face.

Drool poured down and wet my head.

I am not going to make it.

Goodbye my friends.

Goodbye.

48

"Get away from her, you wretched creatures!"

Eva shone a high-intensity discharged beam onto the hordes.

And they immediately backed away like frightened lizards.

They... they are afraid of light?

My whole body was fatigued.

Everything became fuzzy.

My consciousness was floating in an empty space.

I just want to rest.

Before I realized, two pairs of arms grabbed me from behind.

I could barely recognize Sol and Tommy.

They escorted me back to the dropship.

***

"Thank God you are back. I have been worrying about you." Peter wiped his tears away.

"Me too. I miss you. I almost thought I wouldn't make it back to see you," I said.

He cupped his warm hands around mine.

But, the General pulled him away.

"Hey, what is wrong with you? Let me go! " Peter screamed.

"Stay away from her. She might be infected. Right now, she needs to be quarantined and scanned by the medical team first," General Muesel explained.

I gazed at the cold-hearted General.

How can he do that to me? A moment ago, he just wanted to leave me behind. Now, he is trying to separate me from my friends.

I turned to Eva, but she agreed that we needed to be scanned.

The dropship took off.

Soon, we were up in the sky.

I peered outside the window.

The buildings of ED-209 became smaller and smaller, and eventually devoured by mist and fog. Raindrops blurred the window, hammering the metal of our dropship like relentless drumming of nails.

"General, we will reach the atmosphere momentarily. Rough air ahead," the pilot reported.

"Very good. We have retrieved what we need," General Muesel whispered next to Dr. Kim.

The doctor grinned.

I gazed around the dropship.

Beside us, there were no signs of any marines.

"They didn't make it," Eva whispered sadly. "None of them did."

The dropship shook violently as it was hit by debris.

Its hum turned into a metallic shriek.

Lightning cut the sky zig-zag.

"Retro-rockets ready," the pilot said and began to count down.

"5."

"4."

"3."

Then the pilot went silent.

"Mary, what is it? Why stop counting?" General Muesel asked.

Mary didn't reply.

Her pupils dilated.

She pointed at the blurred cockpit with her trembling finger.

She tried to speak but no sound came out.

"Hurry up. Punch the ignition button." General Muesel was annoyed.

Lightning came. Rumbling thunder followed.

A brilliant shock of white cut the sky zigzag, revealing what was lurking in the sky.

PART 7

49

It was the Trinomorph Queen.

It had the color of the night.

"Eva, I cannot believe it! It followed us all the way to the sky," I cried.

Eva swallowed hard.

Another lightning struck.

The creature snarled at us.

It spread its wings and dashed into the sky with full speed.

"Where is it?"

Everyone in the dropship panicked.

"Hit the ignition button now!" General Muesel pushed the pilot aside and went for the button himself.

BANG!

Then the creature collided into our dropship.

It sank its talons into the metal plate of our ship, leaving an ear spluttering sound.

Everything spun.

General Muesel lost his balance and fell over. A box from the top landed on his forehead and knocked him out of consciousness.

"Oh no… we are going down," Molly cried helplessly.

"We are not going to make it…we are going to crash," Karen added.

"No. We will make it out of here," Eva disagreed.

"How do you know?"

"Trust me."

Eva hurried to the pilot seat and took over from Mary.

She pushed the thrust lever to steady the dropship.

I looked around the windows for the signs of the Trinomorph.

But everything outside was inky black.

"Eva, it is prowling behind us!" Peter screamed.

Eva and I gazed at the rear mirror and saw the elongated head of the creature catching up from behind.

The creature lurked closer and closer to our engine.

"Now!"

Without hesitation, Eva punched the retro rocket.

Long orange flames spouted out from below the rocket like a dragon.

Within seconds, the wretched creature was bathed in flames. Its wings melted.

Inhuman shrills echoed in the sky with pain and rage.

"Finally. And very graceful," I uttered a long sigh of relief and gave Eva a thumb up.

"I guess my pilot skills are not very rusty after all." Eva threw me a smile.

50

We were back in Sudoku.

It felt like I was awakened from a nightmare.

Except everything is real.

General Muesel commanded androids onboard to quarantine Hiroyuki.

Dr. Kim had the rest of us go through a series of medical checkups to make sure we are okay before allowing us to sleep in the hypersleep chamber.

"Nova, you are last one," Dr. Kim called my name.

I went inside the medical bay.

The room reminded me of ICU. It was arch shaped, brightly lit. Computers, robotic arms and advanced medical equipment filled the room. In the center of the room was a futuristic medical bed. Above it was a ceiling mounted four-arm set, with each arm holding a flat screen display or spectra LED light.

"Lie down and rest. It won't be long." Dr. Kim smiled.

I took off my shoes and rested on the bed.

Dr. Kim did a couple of scans.

She examined my wounds and applied some antibiotic on it.

"Dr. Kim, can I ask you something?"

"Go ahead."

"How did you and the General know we were in trouble so soon? I heard from Eva that the Chinese unintentionally struck one of their own satellites and caused a chain reaction of debris flying through space. Multiple satellites were down," I asked.

Dr. Kim studied me, as if she was hiding something.

"We didn't. We were not searching for you at first. We were searching for someone else." Dr. Kim faked a smile.

Then I recalled the emails.

General, I am writing to you in case I don't make it back to the interstellar cruiser alive. The chemical, TERA-102100X.141, emitted from Fornax A, is extremely unstable under ambient temperature.

"Are you searching for Dr. Cool?" I guessed.

Dr. Kim paused.

"How do you know?" Dr. Kim finally asked.

"Hiroyuki and I saved his life when he crash landed on Wiur. We were almost swallowed by the giant wave," I said.

"So, you met him?" Dr. Kim queried.

"Yes. I did. He is evil. And - " I said.

Dr. Kim turned to the monitors above her head.

"Hum. You are a lucky one. You are clean," Dr. Kim cut me off.

I was confused.

What does she mean I am the lucky one?

"I beg your pardon?" I asked.

Dr. Kim didn't reply. She showed me a few of the X-rays on her hands.

One of them is from Tommy. Another one is from Peter.

They all had some kind of parasite like thing cradled in a fetus position in their chest.

51

"Th…this is impossible!" I was shocked.

"It is really a miracle that you are not impregnated. But, you will soon be," Dr. Kim mocked.

I jumped up from the medical bay and backed away. Confused.

"Wh…what is going on?" I screamed, feeling betrayed.

Dr. Kim stood up and moved towards me.

"Shhh! The others are in hypersleep chamber. There is no one to save you," Dr. Kim held a finger to her lips.

"Why me?" I cried, took another step back.

"You are just an orphan. No one knows or cares about your existence," Dr. Kim said. "Orphan kids like you are our perfect specimens for our experiment in ED-209. You are so pure. You are so innocent to think we brought you to space to terraform a planet that doesn't exist. The company spends so much money to get you here. They expect results from your body."

"You are insane. You knew about the Trinomorph and you sent us there?" I covered my mouth in disbelief.

"Yes, of course. The debris flying through space and the missions of terraforming Zuptune are all smoke and mirrors. Our real agenda is to lure orphans like you to ED-209. Our main objective is to study the Trinomorph and TERA-102100X.141 so Zirgin Galactic can use them as bio-weapons to win the space race. Everyone on your ship is expendable, even the marines," Dr. Kim revealed.

"You are evil," I accursed. "You orchestrated all this from the beginning!"

"Precisely. But, not exactly. We did not expect Eva to rescue Dr. Cool before us. Otherwise, the general could have his hands on the TERA-102100X.141 sample already. We were already on our way to retrieve our sample. It was Eva who destroyed our plan. It was Eva who ruined everything. It was Eva who told the government about the Trinomorph. That is why we must send her to ED-209 to silence her forever."

"What will you do to my friends?"

"Nothing. We smuggle Trinomorph back through their body." Dr. Kim laughed. "No one will ever find that out."

In the midst of her laugh, all of a sudden, the ship blacked out.

A dying scream sent a shiver down our spines.

That scream….it was loud and clear. It belonged to the General.

"Huh? What is going on?" Dr. Kim began to panic.

She pulled out a pistol from her pocket and searched for the sound.

Without warning, I sneaked behind her in darkness and knocked her down.

Then I took the pistol from her, suited back up in my bulky spacesuit, and raced outside the medical bay.

I ran and ran.

The yellow beacons on the ceiling were flashing for emergency.

Eva? Peter? Where are you?

I turned one corridor after another.

Oh wait. They must be in the sleeping chamber! I must tell them what happened. I must tell them about the company's evil plan. But, how do I get there?

I ran past different places - Cosmetic shops. Hair-dressing shops. Clothing shops. Cinemas. One of them was the Robot kitchen where I ordered my first lasagna in space.

Inhuman hisses filled the ship.

Then I heard Dr. Kim's scream.

I better be quick; otherwise, I will end up being a lasagna myself.

I rushed down one escalator after another until I reached the lobby.

Yes. I remember this place - this giant floor to ceiling window with space view. I think the sleeping chamber is right around the corner.

Just as I was about to exit the lobby, a dark figure dropped from above the ceiling and blocked my way.

52

The humanoid creature stood seven feet tall. It was shaded in black. It had an elongated skull and a skeletal body with biomechanical appearance. The deadliest of all was its unusual long tail with a scorpion like barb.

It… it is impossible.

How…how did it get in our ship?

The only one I saw was the one latching on Hiroyuki's face.

No way it could grew this big. It is just a matter of hours since we boarded Suduko…

Or can it…?

The creature hissed and snarled.

It stood in its hind legs.

Its tail swept back and forth.

Outside the giant glass window was Wiur orbiting Fornax A – the black hole.

I focused on the creature.

You do not belong here. You are a creature manifested from TERA-102100X.141.

I took out the pistol stolen from Dr. Kim and fired

right at it.

Missed.

The creature dodged with great agility and the bullet hit the window instead.

This is no good…

WARNING: ZERO GRAVITY ACTIVATED

Just as the creature was about to counterattack, the A.I. of Sudoku activated the zero gravity.

Ouch!

My body collided with the ceiling.

I was swimming in air again.

The creature reached out for me, but the decompression of the cracked glass sucked it backwards.

BANG!

The creature smashed into the window and glass scattered everything, floating into space.

No! No! No!

I tried to hold onto something, but there was nothing I could grab.

The sucking force was so large.

Everything happened too fast.

Within seconds, I was sucked into space.

53

The whole world was spinning.

I tumbled into space.

The black hole behind me was like a giant monster.

I tried to swim back to the space shuttle with all my strength.

But, no matter how hard I tried, the space shuttle kept drifting further and further away from view.

It felt like an unknown current was pushing back against me in an ocean.

I struggled to swim forward.

This is no good…

It is just a matter of time before I will be completely lost in space.

I began to panic.

My heart was pounding fast.

I was breathing so hard that I could hear it myself.

The water vapor in my breath condensed and blurred my visor.

My hope of returning to Earth was swallowed by despair.

I really want to scream. I really want someone to come and rescue me.

But, the truth is, when you are in space, no one can hear you scream.

The oxygen level in my spacesuit continued to decline.

Nova. Stop wasting time. Quick. Think of something! I urged myself.

"Nova, do you copy?"

A familiar voice with static from the radio interrupted my thoughts.

It was Eva.

"Eva! Eva! Please save me!" I cried.

"Nova, I want you to stop panicking. Tell me what you see," Eva asked.

"I…I can't see anything. I can only see the black hole and planet Wiur," I stammered.

"Are you able to use the jet thruster?" Eva recommended.

"No. Where is the jet thruster?" I asked.

Then the radio went dead silent.

Something interred the signal.

"Hello? Eva, can you hear me? Hello?"

What is happening?

I began to sob.

Suddenly, my radio picked up something else.

It was like an unknown language made up by a series of growls and snarls.

"Hello?"

A colossal shadow overcast my tumbling body.

When I looked up, I could see a mammoth object coming out of the mouth of Fornax A.

Uncloaking.

I dropped my mouth open.

Paralyzed.

A strong beam shone at me.

My body began to accelerate towards the black hole at the speed of light.

"No! No! No!"

55

My whole body was enveloped with light.

I felt warm.

My eyes closed, waiting for whatever was going to happen to me.

It doesn't matter anymore.

At least I am enjoying the last moment of my life.

Distant memories with Mom and Dad came back to me.

I saw the blurred image of myself clapping my little hands, while Mom and Dad were singing birthday songs at me.

Happy birthday to you. Happy birthday to you.

Happy birthday to Nova. Happy Birthday to you.

Hip Hip Hooray.

Mom's musical voice echoed in my thoughts.

Everything looked so real.

Then the blurred began to clear.

There were five candles on my favorite dark forest chocolate birthday cake.

I opened my mouth but no sound came out.

"Sweetheart. It is your five-year-old birthday," Mom smiled.

"Okay, ready? Say cheese and smile," Dad said.

Mom positioned me in the viewfinder frame.

The camera clicked and flashed.

I was overjoyed to see Mom and Dad.

Then I began to cry.

"Sweetheart, what is wrong with you today? It is your birthday." Dad came over to soothe me.

"Mommy, Daddy, I love you. Promise me not to leave. Promise me not to go to space," I hugged them.

"Hey it is okay, sweetheart. We are never going to leave. Mom and I still need to go to work tomorrow, and we still have a mortgage to pay. Where will we ever find time to go to space?" Dad laughed.

"Blow the candles. Make a wish," Mom said.

Is this real?

Just as I lowered my head and began to make a wish, something caught the corner of my eyes.

It was an apple.

What was special about this apple was the two adjacent holes-endowed on the surface on it.

A worm crawled from one hole and then exited from another.

Is this real?

What can I say?

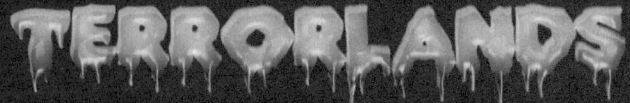

TERRORLANDS

Reader Beaware : You May be in for a scare

MARCO CHU KWAN CHING

About the Author

Marco Chu Kwan Ching's books are read all over the world. Apart from the Terrorlands Series, Marco Chu Kwan Ching is also the author of two books, *Corruption of Real Money* and *Legacy of Debt*.

You can learn more about his work at

www.terrorlands.com

www.corruptionofrealmoney.com

When he is not writing, he loves working on Fiverr. He has thousands of happy customers around the world.

https://www.fiverr.com/mckcvision

Marco Chu Kwan Ching lives in Australia with his wife, Carrie.

Thank you for Reading!

If you love my work, please feel free to leave a positive feedback on Amazon and Goodreads.

My contact:
https://www.facebook.com/marco.chu.10
https://www.goodreads.com/author/show/15944678.Marco_Chu_Kwan_Ching

Terrorlands Facebook Page
https://www.facebook.com/terrorlands/

Terrorlands Twitter Page
https://twitter.com/terrorlands

Goodreads Page
https://www.goodreads.com/book/show/40855316-how-i-got-lost-in-space

Terrorlands Website
http://www.terrorlands.com